KAYLA'S HEAUX TALES

ARNITTRESS DOWDY

KAYLA'S HEAUX TALES

Also, By Arnittress Dowdy

Dreamtini

Dreamtini II: The Reality

Pieces of Me

Simply Me

Kayla's Heaux Tales

KelJam Publishing

ISBN: 979-8-9865099-2-1

This is a work of fiction. Names, characters, places, and incidents are either the product of the author's imagination or used fictitiously. Any resemblance of actual persons, living or dead, events, or locales is coincidental.

Printed in the United States of America

First Edition – June, 2025

Cover Design By BookBrush

ACKNOWLEDGMENTS

Kelvin & James – I love you guys to the moon and back a million times! You two are my heartbeats and my everything. We've hit bumps together and made it over them together. You two keep me going. You two are the best gifts, and I thank you for choosing me to be your mom. Thank you for riding this ride with me and being the best co-pilots.

Juanita Dowdy – I am beyond blessed to have a mother like you. No matter what, you continue to have my back. You've been the most consistent person in my life. I love you, Mommy.

Ronnie Thomas - I may not always say it, but I admire you so much. I am lucky to have a brother like you. Thank you for everything you've done for my boys and me.

Donna Roscoe – My little big sister. I've never said it, but you've helped me in ways that you didn't have to. Not only do I appreciate that, but thank you. Thank you also for allowing me to experience the world. No matter where you've been, you've always made sure that I came to see you.

Lisa Harris – Thirty-plus years, and nothing has changed. I can't thank you enough. You, along with Mommy, have been my biggest cheerleaders, and I appreciate and love you not only for that but also for being a friend. You always remind me why I write, even when I don't feel like it. Thanks, sis.

Ems – You told me that I didn't have to, but I am. Thank you for being an inspiration. Thank you for being that teacher, adult guidance counselor, and the best mentor a person could ever ask for.

CONTENTS

INTRODUCTIONS

Let's meet the players.

Looking back, I've been a sexual being since I was a little girl. But how? In my neighborhood, there were equal numbers of boys and girls. We girls played freeze tag and jumped double dutch. When we included the boys, we played run, catch, and go-get-it, and played house. Both games had the same end result. Dry humping. We would either do it standing up or lying down on the grass. I loved this game. I also loved playing house; depending on who the father would be, I'd volunteer to be the mom. I couldn't have been more than five or six at this time.

I got my first and last ass whopping because of dry humping. Along with three friends, Monica, Robbie, and my "boyfriend," Joey, we were looking for somewhere we wouldn't get caught dry-humping. At this time, my family and I lived in an apartment complex. This complex was on a hill. One building was at the bottom, the second in the middle, and the third on the hill's top. My parents, brother, and I weren't the only ones who lived in this complex. I had an uncle who lived at the bottom and a cousin in the middle. We lived at the top of the hill. Behind the buildings were trees and a long-ass fence- nothing to see. So we couldn't get caught, at least that's what we thought. Little did we know. As we walked past apartment windows, we looked inside to make sure no one was there.

We eventually found a spot behind the second building. It seemed like the perfect spot. But, again, little did we know. Monique and I both lay down on the ground. Robbie got on top of her, and Joey got on top of me. We did what we were on a mission to do: dry hump. Monique and I were dusting the grass off us, and I heard my mom screaming my name. When I looked up, all I could say was, Oh shit, because how did she know that's where I was, and how long had she been standing there?

I could also see that she had something long in her hand. As I got closer, I noticed the long thing in her hand was a belt. But why did she have a belt? I didn't ask or stop. I ran into the apartment, my room, and underneath my bed. When my mom entered the apartment, I heard her calling my name. I saw her feet come into my room and then leave. It was getting dark, and I had to pee, so I had to come from under the bed. I tiptoed to the bathroom, and as I was coming out, my mom caught me and whopped my ass. As I said, that was the first and last ass whopping I ever got. That ass-whopping didn't stop me from dry-humping. I was just extra careful.

Later, I discovered we were in front of my cousin's window. She was getting home from work and decided that her nosey ass needed to look out the window. She had options. She could look out of her bedroom window and only see trees. It wasn't like her front window, where she could see people. Whenever she came home from work, she called my mom, and I guess looking out her window was a part of the routine. That day, she chose to look out her bedroom window, and I think she couldn't believe what she saw. She realized it was me and told my mom. I always wondered if she was already on the phone or had looked out, seen what she saw, and then called my mom. I'll never know.

I remember one day I was at Robbie's house. His mom and my parents were friends. So if I wasn't dry-humping or at my next-door neighbor's house eating, I was at Robbie's. We had just finished lunch, and he was like, "Let's go play." I agreed. So we go into his bedroom and sit on his bed. This is the first time I heard; let me put the tip in. I said, No, we can dry-hump, but you're not putting anything inside me. I could have only been seven at this time. Robbie was either nine or ten.

What the hell did he know about putting the tip in? He did have older brothers, so I guess that's where he could have heard it. But really, put the tip in? Monique was his girlfriend; I wondered if he had asked her, and she said no, so that's why he asked me. Who knows? Robbie insisted he put the tip in, and once he realized I was adamant about my no, he stopped asking. Somehow, he convinced me to at least dry hump with our pants down. We did. It felt funny. It felt like something wiggly on top of my precious flower, and then it froze up. At least, that's the way I could describe it. I'm laughing because we were fucked up friends as I think back.

Monique was his so-called girlfriend, and Joey was my so-called boyfriend, and they did everything together. Where there was Robbie, there was Joey, and vice versa. But we were young, so whatever. Later that year, my mom and dad divorced, and my mom, brother, and I moved. The new friends I made weren't into dry-humping; well, they were, but this would be considered dry-hump rape as I think back. Since I was the new kid on the block, they had to put me through some shit. In school, it was all gravy. When we played tag, the boys would touch the girls' butts, and the girls would kiss the boy they caught on the cheek. We eventually got in trouble for that. The principal called our parents. My mom didn't beat me for this. Thank goodness! Now back to the dry-hump rape.

In school, everything was all gravy. We'd get on the bus and head to the seats in the back. Once we were far from the school, someone would grab my arms and legs and lay me in the seat, and this boy would get on top of me against my will. I enjoyed dry-humping, but not this way. But if we called the SVU department, Benson and Stabler would classify this as dry-hump rape. I'd try to fight to get loose, but nope. This continued until I got smart enough to sit closer to the driver in the front. Then they picked on someone new. I never reported it because I didn't want to know what the consequences would be. Now that I'm thinking about it, right before we moved, in second grade, a girl forced a boy and me into the bathroom and told us that we had to dry-hump to come out. She watched through the cracked door. Would that also be considered dry-hump rape? Was I dry-humped raped twice? Anyway, after moving and not having any friends to volunteer for dry-humping, I began to miss dry-humping, so I got creative. Since I was missing dry-humping, I created a fake body. I'd stuff my dirty clothes into a pair of sweatpants, making sure there was a bulge, put a shirt over one of my big teddy bears, and hump away. It gave me the same stimulation as dry-humping with a boy.

When we moved, we moved into a house. My brother's room was upstairs. My room was downstairs, across the hall from my mother. Outside of my mother's bedroom door was a closet. Her clothes, nail polish, shoes, pocketbooks, and porn stash were in this closet. I was a nosey kid. When she was gone, I'd always look in her closet. One night, she went out with a friend, and I went through her collection. I had my own television and VCR in my room. I grabbed two tapes. One was an all-black cast, and the other was an all-white cast. The black pornos, for some reason, I didn't like them, and to this day, I still don't watch them in my forties. I enjoy big booty and big tittie girl-on-girl porn.

My brother never checked on me. Everyone knew I was either listening to music or watching television in my room with the door closed. Once I popped the tape into the VCR, pressed play, and watched the porn stars perform oral sex and have sex. I was turned on. I started throbbing between my legs. I noticed how one of the men rubbed on the actress's pink pearl, and I began to rub my little clitoral flower the same way. I started off slow, eventually picking up the pace. My clit started pulsing as my heart raced. It felt so good; a certain feeling would come over me, and then I'd stop. I realized I was stopping before I could orgasm when I got older.

So basically, I started dry-humping at five and began playing solo with my flower at age nine. Of course, most girls were into dolls and whatever else, but my ass was already interested in sex. I was never any boy's first choice, never an option to get with in junior high and high school. I was always the "friend."

I never had the birds-and-the-bees conversation. I mean, I was never told about the birds and the bees. Instead, I learned everything about sex by watching after-school specials, health classes, my mom's trusty old porn collection, and hearing friends talk about their experiences. So when I eventually told my mom that I had sex, no matter how I answered, it wasn't right. I told her months after my first boyfriend and I broke up. To her, it sounded recent. When she asked where it happened, I told her it was at a hotel; she said he took me there like a prostitute. I wanna say that she hoped I wasn't disrespecting his parents' house before asking where it happened.

So, as you can see, it wasn't right either way. Little did she know it was in her home. To this day, I regret ever telling her. I was looking for how you feel, and now you need to be put on birth control conversation, but that didn't happen. The next day, my dad called to speak to me, and I heard her tell him, you know your daughter is out there fucking. WOW! When I got on the phone, his first thing was, you know, you can catch an STD? We used a condom, but yes, and I'm fine.

Once my older brother knew I was having sex, he gave me the big brother-little sister talk. He taught me how guys think and act, and how I should respond in certain situations. He taught me how to play the "game."

Once I mastered the art of having sex, whoever I was attracted to sexually could get it. If I were in a relationship, if the sex was good, that's all I wanted to do. We didn't have to go out; it didn't have to be a special occasion. If he wanted to fuck, I WAS DOWN!

My name is Kayla, and I thoroughly enjoy sex.

This sounds crazy, but she knew me and didn't completely understand me. She knew that when I was pleased, it made her feel good. But she didn't know she had to follow through with pleasing me until she got older. So, technically, I was never really pleased. I would get there, and then she'd stop. But I must admit that her attention made me feel good. She learned about me and my capabilities in Health class. After learning more about me, I wondered if she fully understood me. She couldn't stand me when she became familiar with my mood swings. She hated how I made her feel.

Not all the time, but sometimes. Kayla would catch an attitude and not know why, or get very emotional and not know why. I would get bloody mad, or what she likes to call bitchy, for three to seven days. I'd get frustrated before these mood swings because I needed to be touched or pleased. All I knew was I needed someone to pay attention to me, and I didn't care who it was. Just stroke my damn ego. Once I feel good and my red mood passes, I must be stroked, or an accommodating thrashing once or twice would be nice. These mood swings of mine only came every thirty or ninety days. I was a little off. I didn't get on track until she was about twenty-five.

Initially, she didn't fully understand me, but she knew me. However, she loved it when the worst side came through. It was a bit confusing; she had a love-hate relationship with the worst side of me. Eventually, she learned I was mighty and could make any man or woman extraordinarily emotional and crazy. She pleased me as she continued learning about me, ensuring I was delighted.

I must admit that I've gotten her into some trouble, but it wasn't anything she couldn't handle. Although we now have a deal, sometimes she leads, and other days I take over. But I can tell you one thing, on the days I take the lead, she's never disappointed. We were suitable for the first sixteen years because I let her control our relationship. She was in two long-term relationships where "everything" was equally good. Still, the day she allowed me to maintain the connections came. From that day forward, we would have whatever men she saw that made ME throb. So naturally, we had some fun days and some emotional days. The best days not only left us speechless, but also kept us thinking about them weeks later. To most people, I go by Vagina and Pussy. **I go by Kay-Kay to my friend Kayla; these are our tales.**

OUR TALES

There's a difference between a smart heaux and a dumb heaux. A smart heaux never tells people her business and ensures she doesn't play in her backyard. A dumb heaux doesn't care who knows her business or where she plays. Sometimes, I can be an unsmart heaux, but not because people know my business, which they don't. But unsmart heaux, meaning not an intelligent player.

THE FIRST TIME

I had been masturbating since I was nine, and here I was, fourteen, with a sixteen-year-old boyfriend. After five years of masturbating, it was definitely time to have sex. I can't imagine or don't know how long Derrick had been masturbating, but I know he wasn't washing his hair in those long-ass showers he took. Our mothers were really good friends, so they had no problem with us being boyfriend and girlfriend. When they went out, we'd spend time together, so it made sense, along with the fact that he liked me more than a friend and didn't see me as one of the guys or his "little" sister. The fact that I was crushing on him, too, also helped. I remember our mothers planned to go to a concert, and Derrick was coming over to spend the night. So I figured I'd ask him if he wanted to watch a porno, I'd watch him and see what it did to him, and then ask him if he wanted to try what the actors were doing? When he got to my house, I soon discovered we were on the same page.

Knocking on the door, "Kayla, you in there?"

"Come in." I was lying on the bed watching television. "What's up?" I asked as I got up to give him a hug.

"You know they're gonna be gone all night, right?"

"Yes, I do, which means you're spending the night."

"So, what are we going to do?"

"What you wanna do?"

"Kayla!" my mom said as she knocked and opened the door.

"Yes?"

"We are leaving. You two behave."

"Yes, ma'am." We walked my mom out of my room, watched our mothers get into the car and drive off, then returned to my room.

I brought my attention back to Derrick. "So what you wanna do?" I asked.

"To be honest, Kay, I'm tryna get up in that."

Shocked and turned on simultaneously, "Is that right?"

"Yes, it is. And I know you're ready. So let's stop playing games and take this relationship to the next level."

Curiously, "Do you know what you're doing?"

"I've heard my friends talk about it."

"So that means no."

Laughing, "I have watched pornos, so I do know."

"No, you don't, but I can pop one in, and we can watch and learn together." The tape was already in the VCR; I had to hit the play button.

"So, you already had a porno in the VCR?"

Laughing, "Mind your business, but if you must know, I put this in before you arrived. I had a plan."

Shocked, "And what was your plan?"

As a matter of fact, "I'm ready to have sex, and I figured I'd try to see if you wanted to watch a porno, and I'd watch you. Problem with that?" Did I say that? Was it normal for a girl to say something like that? Yeah, I said it, and it was my normalcy.

Shaking his head, "Nope."

"Good, now shut up, and let's watch." He sat at the end of the bed. I pressed play on the remote while lying in bed. I became aroused as the actor kissed the actress and played with her pussy. I could feel a throbbing sensation between my legs. I looked over at Derrick, and he was watching me. The next thing I knew, he moved and lay down behind me. I was wearing his basketball shorts; he rubbed my thigh, went underneath the shorts, and began rubbing on my moist mound as he kissed my neck.

"Oh, so you're already turned on?" He asked.

I couldn't respond; I felt his finger go inside me, and then I felt two. As he kissed me on my neck, I turned my head so that we were face to face. We kissed passionately, and I moved with the motion of his fingers. As it was getting hot, he stopped, went into his pocket, pulled out a condom, pulled down his sweatpants and boxers in one shot, and put the condom on his rigid member. He put me on my back and got on top of me; he spread my legs apart with his legs. With his dick in his hand, he moved the tip up and down on my clit. Once he got to the entrance, he put the tip in. I took a deep breath and closed my eyes. It didn't hurt, as I heard from my friends who were having sex.

Something was trying to penetrate me. However, it seemed as if it was hard to enter me. It was slow, going in and out of me until it was finally inside me. Once I was used to the in-and-out motion, it moved in a circular motion. As I got used to that, it went back to the ramming. I was profusely sweating during the different movements. I mean, I was thoroughly soaked. It was like the sweat was building up. By the time I got into the flow of things, it was like the sword had gone limp, and it was over. That experience lasted, oh, let's say, about ten minutes at the most. But what happened next.....OH MY!!! The sword eased out of me, and the owner came down to personally meet me. It was like I became his favorite lollipop. He slowly licked my entrance; he freely moved his tongue over me. With all of me inside his mouth, he moved his tongue from side to side.....WHEW!!! Like the sword, his tongue stabbed the hell out of me correctly. The best part was when his tongue became stiff, and he would do the worm. He would catch me off guard every time he switched up his movements. He did that until her legs began to shake, and soon after, her body started to jerk, and the sweat had built up to the point where I couldn't hold it in. And just like the sword, I exploded; however, my explosion was like water shooting out of a hydrant. What the fuck? Did I piss in this boy's mouth? (We later learned that was an s-orgasm, aka squirting orgasm)

When Derrick's tongue fucked me, I fucked the shit out of his face to the best of my ability. I could hear him moaning right along with me. I got to the point where when I masturbated, I'd start throbbing and then stop, but I didn't want him to, and he didn't. As he continued to tongue fuck me, I fucked his face, my legs started shaking, and my body started to jerk. In my head, I was like, Oh shit! I've read about orgasms, but didn't think I'd have one my first time. Derrick actually knew what the fuck he was doing. The next thing I know, I hear slurping noises. Then he stopped.

"I told you I know what to do."

"How, Derrick? How did you know what to do?" I asked, out of breath.

"My dad talked with me, and my godbrother also hit me off with pornos. So you are not the only one watching porn."

I couldn't help but laugh. "How do you feel?"

"I feel good. I busted a nut and made you bust one. So I'm good. How do you feel?"

"Shit, I could do it again if you're up to it. But if you're not, I can wait until tomorrow."

"Oh, you're saying we can add sex to our relationship now?"

"Fuck. Yes," and I was so serious.

After our first time, Derrick and I would have sex at every chance. When he and his mom would come over, he and I would go downstairs to the basement and pretend to watch TV. We'd open up the windows and fuck. When he got his car, it was a wrap. We'd find spots, park the car, and fuck in the car.

Derrick and I were together until he graduated and went off to college. I'd go visit him, and we would have sex, and of course, when he came home, we'd fuck. We went from boyfriend and girlfriend to fuck buddies when we broke up. During my senior year in high school, I fucked with one guy, Jamal. We had a love-hate relationship. As I look back then, we had a toxic relationship. We'd physically fight, smoke weed, and then fuck. It wasn't good one day. On this one day, in particular, he almost threw me down a flight of stairs, and later that evening, I almost threw him through a barbershop window. A customer and a barber saved him. I don't know where the strength came from, but I yoked him by his jacket and was about to put him through the window when the customer and barber saved him. About an hour later, we smoked, laughed, and fucked. We continued this toxic relationship until my first year in college.

My first year of college was done; I was home and on a fuck mission. I was going to have sex as often as possible. I had two options: I could continue to fuck Jamal, aka Mr. Toxic, or go on a fucking spree. If dick was thrown at or offered to me, I wouldn't turn down the dick. If a guy could fuck as many girls as he wanted to, why couldn't I fuck as many guys as I wanted and not be labeled a heaux? But, of course, I had to be discreet, and I knew that the neighborhood guys weren't options. One thing —well, one of the things—I learned about guys by hanging out with them is that they like to gossip. So, to not be known as Kayla the heaux or be the topic of conversation, I always kept to myself, which meant nobody knew my business. I didn't live too far outside New York City, where I went to college, so I'd find dick. If I couldn't get into the city, I'd smoke weed and discreetly dabble within the hood.

How the local guys treated some of the girls they fucked with is how I treated them. And I ensured it was always a one-time thing with the locals if I dabbled in my backyard. My male best friend, Breezy, said to me, Kayla, I could never fuck with you. I asked him why not. His reply was that I treat dudes like bitches. I had to ask him what he meant by that. I knew, but I just wanted to confirm my assumption.

He told me that guys only want one thing from a chick, and that's pussy, and after they get that, they don't want to be bothered, and that's how I treated the guys from around the way. You get dick and keep it moving. He was right, and my assumption was correct. He then went on to tell me which one of the street dudes I fucked. How? He told me he noticed that when I came around, they acted differently. He also said he saw that I made it clear I gave zero fucks when they talked to me. And of all people, Breezy knew when I didn't want to be bothered with a mothafucka.

Remember, he's one of my best friends. Breeze's mom and my mom were friends and worked together. So anytime their company had a picnic, Breeze and I would hang out. When we were little, we'd play together if a park was nearby, and as we got older, we began to talk more. We automatically labeled ourselves best friends because we trusted each other enough to share our secrets and speak about everything from relationships to sex, school, and sports. Breeze was my dude; I could always count on him if I was in trouble or needed help. And vice versa

I remember him saying, before I would come around, those dudes are all tough, but when they see you, heyyy, Kayla. It's like the street leaves them, and the bitch in them emerges. And they know we are cool, so they keep asking me about you. Mothafuckas sprung off one hit, and you keep it moving, not giving a fuck. I know they must feel like bitches because I feel bad for them. I'm laughing on the inside like, yeah, y'all meet y'all match. I'm not trying to feel like no bitch. And that, my friend, is why I could never fuck you.

That fucked me up, but at the same time, he was right; I didn't give a fuck. As my brother told me, if I wanted to play the game, I needed to be the best player and not the game. So that's what I was doing. And not for nothing, I heard some chicks talk about how good some of those hood guys were. HUH?! These mothafuckas were trash. I remember my childhood friend Monique was head over heels in love with this one guy. I remember going with her to get a hotel room for them and helping her make it all romantic. She always talked about how good his dick was.

I had another friend who did the same thing, but asked me to get a room for them. She also claimed his dick was good. I didn't think three years later I'd be fucking him and asking myself what kind of dick they were getting, cause that mothafucka one was trash, and two didn't last long. His dick was small, and he lasted three minutes. He blamed it on the Hennessey he drank. And not for nothing, while he was drinking, his ass was popping the most shit. My high ass was like ok, what's up? After the three minutes, I got dressed and left. After that one time, he would ask for another try at it every time he saw me. Boy, bye.

I would get myself into some situations when I smoked. When I smoked naturally, I'd get high and hungry, but I also got horny. When I get horny(smh), I take a chance. I end up fucking someone I wouldn't fuck sober. I remember finding out some crazy shit about me. I saw someone I grew up with, but our circles were different. When she saw me, she said, I need to talk to you. All I could think was, what the fuck could she possibly have to speak to me about? We both had family living in the complex where we grew up and visited. I sat down on the step next to her, and she told me a guy she refused to name told her that I had jumped out of some guy's window. I sat there and really thought about it. Like, was I that high that I did some shit like that? If I had to think about it, it definitely wasn't me. If I came through the front door, I left through the front door. But someone did jump out of my window after eating my pussy. We'll call him Curt; I knew Curt's older brother and father. Every time Curt saw me, for some reason, he would ask to eat my pussy, and I would always play it off and tell him one day. One day came.

My mom had company, but they were downstairs, so it was easy to sneak him in. We entered my room; he pushed me down on the bed, removed my pants, and ate my pussy. That was it. No foreplay, no fucking; he went straight to licking and sucking. He was good, I must admit. I went to the bathroom and saw my mom and her friends in the living room. I returned to my room and told Curt he had to leave, and he went out the window. My room was on the second floor, but the window wasn't that high from the ground. You could easily jump out, but you need a ladder to get through it from the outside. Curt looked out the window and said, "Okay." So I told him to hang and then jump, which he did.

Days later, word on the street was that I sucked his dick. Breeze and I were sitting on the block, and he asked me. And I told him no and asked who told him that, and he said that's what Curt was saying. Five minutes later, Breeze tapped me on my leg and pointed in Curt's direction. Curt was walking up the block; Breeze and I were drinking Heinekens. I had just finished mine. I grabbed the bottle by the neck, approached Curt, and addressed the rumor. He swore up and down that he didn't say that. I said okay and walked away. I was ready to bust him upside his head with that bottle. That was the only jumping-out-of-the-window story that I knew of that included me. But according to old girl, the person whose window I allegedly jumped out of was Jamal (Mr. Toxic). She knew he and I messed around. She also mentioned that Jamal was having a baby. Did she expect me to tell on myself regarding my involvement with him? Not today, tomorrow, or yesterday will she get a reaction from me. For that moment, my response was, I continued with my oh wows, oh really, and hmphs.

When she was done, I said, "Wow, that wasn't me," and I wish Mr. Toxic all the best with his baby and baby momma. So I got up, said bye, and went on my way. A few days later, I ran into Mr. Toxic and saw that he was expecting a baby. It was only the summer. We had been fucking since my senior year of high school; he didn't have a girlfriend, and he spent damn near all summer at my house before I left for school. Even when I went to school, he was my overnight guest every other weekend. He stopped visiting when he saw I was too friendly with one of the basketball players right before I went on Spring Break. He didn't like that. Besides, I was only interested in dick; I wasn't looking to be in or did I want a relationship, and he knew that. So why would he lie about having a girlfriend? Why didn't he tell me he was having a baby? On the night of finding out about the baby on the way, I went to a local bar for a few drinks. Yes, I was underage, and the bartenders didn't care. I walked home to find out I didn't have my keys. I had them when I left home. I went all the way back to the bar, but nobody found the keys. So I walked the same route back home and found them on the grass in front of a church. After picking them up, I saw this dude with his baby momma, who looked like she was about to pop. As he stopped to talk to me, he told her to keep walking. Who does that? She kept walking. I asked him who she was, and he said, "My baby's momma." I then asked when she was due, and he said in a few days. I'm not good at math, but I quickly did the math and told him that he needed to catch up to her. His dick wasn't that good and not worth the drama. Oh well! But damn!!! But he was mad at me for being too friendly, and he had a baby on the way…smdh. After that, I ended up fucking another local, Rick, who was a very late-night creep. I'm talking about nobody on the streets; I can walk without looking for a shortcut, so I don't bump into anyone. This local's dick was so good that before I left his house, I asked him for a cigarette; I took two and smoked them on my way home, or to Breeze's house, or my Tionne, my female best friend. My smoking cigarettes was rare because I was a pothead. We fucked a few more times before it was time for me to return to school, and that was it. After that, we'd bump into each other, have a quick conversation, and keep it moving. Which was how it was supposed to be.

TRAIN WRECK

We were out of our comfort zone and in a place we would not return to. This was the first episode in which Kayla allowed me total control. Kayla had just finished her second year in college. She went to Georgia to visit a relative instead of going home for winter break. On our third day in Georgia, Kayla looked through the window over the kitchen sink when she spotted Derek and Adam. Derek stood about five feet nine inches tall, with an athletic build, and had some pretty hazel-green eyes. Adam was about 5'10 ", muscular, with a mocha complexion. To Kayla, he was decent-looking. Nothing really stood out. Well. At least not, then. Kayla's brains and eyes, and I communicate; that's how I know what they looked like, just in case you're wondering.

"Hey, who are they?" She asked Kim before she headed out. Kim's mom and Kayla's mom were close friends, making Kayla and Kim "cousins." Kim was a few years older than Kayla and always acted like her older sister. Kayla loved that because she had an older brother and couldn't talk to him about female things.

"Oh, that's Derrick and Adam. They're cousins who are actually about your age. Would you like me to introduce you to them?" She asked as she grabbed Kayla's arm along with her car keys. "Adam! David! Come here for a second." She yelled.

"Did I really have a choice?" Kayla asked through her smile.

"Not really. Adam, Derrick, this is my cousin Kayla."

Shaking their hands, "Hi, Derrick. Hello, Adam."

"Kayla is here from New York; she'll be here for two weeks. Since you are all the same age, you two could show her around?"

"Well, we were about to go to the mall. You're more than welcome to come with us." Adam said, smiling.

"Kim is on her way out, and I must watch her son. Maybe another time."

"He can come along." David said with a huge grin, "He's my little dude."

"See, it all works out. You enjoy yourself, and I'll go back in and send Shawn out with your pocketbook." "Sure," Kayla said.

Once Shawn came outside, they packed into the Honda Accord and headed to the mall. Unfortunately, the mall they went to had nothing to brag about, one floor with many stores and a food court. Kayla found a sneaker store and bought a pair of sneakers for her and Shawn. Kayla always wanted a little brother or sister. Since she was attached to Kim when she was pregnant with Shawn seven years ago, once Shawn was born, she treated him like her little brother. Kayla babysat him for free. She spoiled him; whenever she shopped for herself, she'd always find and mail something for him. After they had done a little shopping, they headed home.

"You know if you aren't doing anything later, Kayla, you can stop by," David said from the backseat.

"Maybe I will." Adam pulled into Kim's driveway to let Kayla and Shawn out.

"So, how was it?" Kim eagerly asked as Kayla and Shawn walked in.

"You know what your mall is like, and I'm pretty sure you've been there a gazillion times. You should have an idea."

"You're such a smart-ass. I meant Derrick and Adam."

"I don't know, but Derrick invited me over later."

After dinner and everyone had turned in for the night, Kayla decided to go across the street to see what Derrick and Adam were about. They were already sitting in the garage, drinking. "Hey, Kayla, you want a drink?" Derrick asked.

"Sure, whatcha got over there?" She asked, making herself comfortable on one of the lawn chairs.

"We have some Absolut and your choice of Cranberry or Orange juice," Adam said, smiling with his eyes.

"I'll have the Cranberry juice." He handed her a drink, and this was when I took over. After a few drinks and talking, we entered the family room inside the house. They all got comfortable on the floor and started a friendly conversation about sex. The next thing I knew, the Absolut and Cranberry kicked in. Alcohol kicks in the same way the weed does, except instead of being high, she's a little tipsy, and nothing's enhanced. Everybody's hands were all over each other. Kayla was experienced but not experienced, but I thought, why not? We wouldn't be speaking or seeing these guys again, and who would know besides us four? All of a sudden, I felt somebody stroking me. As I was being tickled, Kayla's breasts were being rubbed on. Then, I felt a finger moving around inside of me. Kayla had a dick in each hand. As I said, we weren't that experienced. She already had it in her head that she wasn't putting anything in her mouth, and luckily, no one asked or attempted to.

Adam's dick was the first to get hard, so he bent her over and entered. His dick made up for what he was lacking in looks. Adam was thrusting me for a good fifteen minutes. There were moments when she had to stop jerking David off because the thrusting felt good, and she wanted to get into it. Instead, I did the trick. I grip a dick and make it hard for the owner to slide in and out. I noticed that it drives the owners crazy, and they go limp quick. This happened to Adam. After he came, he went to sucking her breasts, and David went behind, and after two minutes, he was done. And I didn't even get to do the trick on him. So the two minutes were disappointing. Good looks and a two-minute brother. Adam put on another condom, and he lasted a good ten minutes. As soon as he entered, I gripped that dick. Adam seemed to work with the trick. Derrick came back for another two minutes. After he was done, Kayla quickly got up and got dressed. All that fucking, and I didn't cum. Wasn't that a bitch?! They walked her back across the street. Adam kissed her on the cheek and told her she had some good pussy. Trust me, she's learning. David told her he would be back in the morning. We both hoped the fuck not. After we showered, we got in bed and lay there. Kayla started talking to herself.

"Is that what a menage a trois is about? I don't think so. There was no oral sex, and from the pornos I've seen, what we did wasn't like that. Maybe I'll try it again when I'm older and more experienced. That

was probably what they call a train, but it was a train wreck. I also hope the doorbell doesn't ring in the morning because I won't answer it. Tonight was definitely one for the books.

Everyone was gone, and I was the only one in the house. I got up and made myself breakfast. Someone knocked at the door just as I was about to clean the kitchen. I could see through the curtain that it was David. I quietly put the dishes in the sink, dropped to the floor, and crawled to my room. David rang the doorbell for a good five minutes before leaving. When he left, the house phone started ringing. I know damn well he didn't have the house's number, buuuuut I wasn't going to pick up the phone. Finally, the answering machine picked up, and I could hear it was David. I eventually saw him when I took out the garbage later that day. Thank goodness Kim and Shawn came outside and hopped in the car. That was my cue. I avoided him and his cousin for the rest of my stay. I couldn't wait to get back home.

A few years after this experience, I had another similar but slightly different one. I grew up with George, and I knew Sam. I didn't think they were related. But, after hanging out with them a few times, I eventually discovered they were cousins. One night, I was at George's house, and we were smoking. We lay on the bed and watched television, and one thing led to another. He was behind me. He tried entering Kay-Kay from behind, but it wouldn't go in. He'd go limp every time he tried to enter, but he eventually entered. As he was pumping in and out, I felt disgusted. I was horny but not horny for him. I told him to stop, and I got up and put on my clothes. He asked me what was wrong, and I told him it didn't feel right that we shouldn't be having sex. He was a little confused by that because he thought we were okay. After getting dressed, I left, and Sam caught me and offered me a ride home. I took the ride, but we ended up back at his place. We smoked, and I told him what had happened between his cousin and me. We laughed, and the next thing I knew, my clothes were off again, and we were fucking. First, I was on top; then he was; then he hit it from the back. Sex was decent, but I'd never do him again. I couldn't believe what had happened, but it happened. Whenever George and Sam see me, they give me that 'so when are we gonna fuck again?' look. I laugh and keep it moving like nothing ever happened.

GROWING PENIS

Kayla had known Nathan since they were seven years old. They attended the same summer camp and became great friends. As they got older, they eventually became camp counselors at the same camp. After the counselor's parties, they would go for ice cream. They lived in different towns but had mutual friends and hung out at the same places. After camp, they continued their ice cream dates every other Saturday. However, it wasn't until after high school that things began to heat up between them.

Whenever Kayla and Nathan hung out, they would talk. I mean, how much talking can two people do? Since they were seven, they have known each other, so twelve years of speaking should be enough talking. I could sense the sexual attraction between them, but for some reason, they couldn't. It was frustrating for me. Then came this one weekend. They both came home from college every weekend and always hung out; it was routine. But this one weekend, in particular, was different. It was a Friday, a lovely spring night, and they were sitting on Kayla's mother's deck having a beer. Naturally, there was that damn conversation. But, I must admit, this conversation was different from the rest.

"How come we never got together, Kay?" Nathan asked as he took a sip of his beer.

"Excuse me?" She asked, shocked. Kayla always saw Nathan as someone she could be in a relationship with if she weren't with Derrick, but she valued their friendship. Of course, he probably could have been someone she just fucked, but she loved their friendship, and also, Mr. Toxic's dick was good enough then.

"I'm pretty sure you have deep feelings for me, and I can admit that I did and still do for you. We've spent our summers together, working at the summer camp, having lunch, and attending camp parties. Even the times we spent together during high school, hanging out with and without our mutual friends."

She couldn't believe what she had just heard. Well, at least now she knew the feeling was mutual. Damn, to think, Nathan could have been dipping his stick inside of me. "Well, why didn't you say anything to me before?" She asked as she cleared her throat.

"I don't know. Maybe because I was scared, I didn't know how you would react. I wanted to say something our senior year, but I found out you were fucking with Jamal(Mr Toxic)."

"Oh wow! Why are you bringing this up now?"

"It was on my mind, that's all." Looking down at his watch. "Damn, I hate that I started this conversation now because I gotta go. Dinner with the family. Walk me to my car." He grabbed their beer bottles and led the way. He dropped the bottles in the recycling bin as they headed toward the front of the house. "Well, Kayla, seeing you is always a pleasure. And I apologize for starting a conversation that I can't finish," He said, turning to her.

"Same here. So when do you leave? " She asked, trying not to look him in the eyes.

"Sunday, but tomorrow is Saturday, and it's Sundae Nite for us. So I'll be back for you tomorrow night at 8." He leaned in to give her a hug.

Hugging him back, she said, "Okay, see you tomorrow night." She didn't wait for him to pull off to go inside; she ran into the house, straight to her bedroom, and fell face-first onto her bed. She rolled over on her back and thought about what Nate had said. She liked him more than a friend, but the friendship meant more. Could the friendship strengthen the relationship? What if it didn't work out as boyfriend and girlfriend? Would they still have been able to remain the good friends that they were? While thinking about the conversation, we fell asleep. She kept busy all day Saturday. That night, they went out for their sundaes. No one brought up the conversation from the night before, and we got a kiss at the end of the night. Yes, a measly fucking kiss. It wasn't that bad. He used just enough tongue and lips, not too wet and far from sloppy. It was one of those kisses that led to the bedroom. It took us to the bedroom. Alone.

Their next home visit was going to be something entirely different. They actually made plans, dinner, and then sundaes. In her mind, she kept replaying the kiss over and over again. Hopefully, she'd convince him to come inside since she knew her mom was leaving town. Amid her thoughts, Nate called her. After their conversation, she headed into the shower to do some maintenance. Kayla paid real close attention to me, making sure I looked presentable. Thursday, she went to class and worked with Friday on her brain. Friday morning, she woke up excited about Nate's phone call. Shit, we were both excited. "Hello."

"I'll be at your house around six to pick you up for dinner."

"Not a problem." *After she hung up, she showered and went to her two classes. She brought her overnight bag to her classes. After her last class, all she had to do was hop on the train to the bus that would get her home in an hour. Once she got home and settled in, she relaxed for a minute and began getting ready.*

He was on time, and dinner was great. After dinner, I started taking over. He was always a sucker for Kayla's massages, which got him inside. When they got to her bedroom, he took off his shirt and lay on her bed. She went to work on his honey-coated athletic body. He had a chiseled chest, beautiful abs, and a peek-a-boo line to die for. She slowly and sensually massaged his back; she told him to turn over so that she could rub the front of his body. Now, as she was sitting on top of him, I felt nothing. So, I encouraged her a little more. She leans in and begins to nibble on his ear as he touches her breasts and is close enough to kiss her neck; as he holds her, he forces himself to sit up, and he continues kissing her on her neck, making his way to her earlobe. Okay, now we are getting somewhere, but still, I feel nothing. His top is off; her top is off. They are both sitting up; he unsnaps her bra and throws it on the floor. He's now holding her breasts in his hands. He's licking, biting, sucking, and teasing. As I'm getting wet, still, I feel nothing.

She pushes him on his back and begins to kiss and lick his body all over. Please don't ask how it happened, but both his and her pants came off. He's in his boxers, and she's in her thong. I send her a signal to put her hands in his boxers. She feels for something but can't seem to find it. She knows it's there, but where? Finally, she feels a little something in her hands. We are both like, "Oh, hell no." Then the strangest thing happens.

As she began to play with it, it grew. Finally, it reached the size most penises are before erection, and then it was fully erect. Hark, I hear angels singing. He grabs for a condom and puts it on. We are still not experienced, but we have used what we learned. With her on her knees but on top, she went up and down as he held her hips, fast and slow, moving in a circular motion. She'd go up so that only the tip was in before she slid down. She got up while still on top, putting her feet by his side and her hands behind her. We worked it out as she bounced up and down on his dick; this was something she remembered from watching pornos. We were doing the damn thing! He flipped her on her back so that he was now on top. He had her pinned to the bed with her legs up in the air, and as he pumped in and out of me, I would tighten up. These bodies worked until they were sweaty. He exploded before I could, but kept going, so I could also explode. So thoughtful.

After they finished, they scrambled to get dressed. Kayla and Nate talked for a bit. Again, nobody cares about their conversation; that's all they did. Then, she walked him to his car, and they kissed goodnight. Before he left, they promised each other that what took place wouldn't ruin their friendship. The next day was Saturday, meaning Sundae night now has extra toppings.

Nathan and I continued Sundae night for about a year. Some Fridays, we would fuck, but Saturday was still Sundae night, occasionally with extra sprinkles. Toward the end of the year, we were drifting apart. We missed each other's phone calls and made excuses not to meet. Our relationship changed, and we could see it. But we didn't know how to fix it or talk about it. So, I guess we figured drifting apart was better…..LESSON LEARNED: Never add sex to a perfect friendship when you're not ready to deal with the emotions that come with it. I also think he wanted something more and said nothing, and he saw that my actions showed that I was just tryna fuck. Sometimes, when you're friends, that's the way it should stay. Friends who talk about anything can hang out and have a great time together.

I DON'T FEEL ANYTHING

I knew Harold from around the way. I often hung out at the local barbershop. Harold would tell me how he could tear my ass up. Of course, it wasn't anything new since I'd always have some guy trying to holla at me so they could try to tap "dat ass." Still, I never gave in unless I was high, couldn't get into the city, and was bored. On this particular day, it had been snowing, and it finally stopped, but I was stuck locally. It was my last weekend home, so I visited a friend before returning to school. I walked to her house and smoked a blunt; I stopped at the barbershop since it was on the way. When I walked in, I said hello to everyone and sat down. Why did I sit next to Harold?

"What's up, Kayla? Where are you headed or coming from?"

"Hey Harold, I'm headed up the block. Why?"

"Just being nosey." He said, laughing. "Can I ask you a question?"

"What?" I'm expecting the tall girl's question.

"Is what they say about tall women true?"

I knew it. "I don't know, Harold, I don't have a penis to fuck a tall woman? But humor me, what do they say?" I've heard this question more than a hundred times.

"They say tall women are deep. But you know me, I don't care; I'll still tear that ass up."

I'm about six feet two inches tall, slim, thick in the waist, and busty. I have a lot of men who are curious about how deep I am, so what Harold asked me was nothing new. "Again, I don't have a dick, so I don't know if that's true."

Cutting her off, "Alright, Kayla. So can I find out?"

"Can you beat it up as you day?" What was I thinking? I couldn't be serious; there was no way I was thinking about what I thought I was thinking. That weed I smoked had me tripping for real.

"Yes." He said with an even bigger smile.

"Let's go." Yes, I was thinking about it. Why? Harold was not that attractive, and he came up to my chin. I was twenty, and he was in his thirties, with a forty-year-old dad body trying to keep up with the younger guys. We hopped in his car and drove to his place. He lived with his parents. We went upstairs to his room. I sat on the bed, and he sat down next to me. Our coats came off; he lifted my shirt and started caressing my breasts. It did nothing.

The next thing I know, I'm on my back, waiting for him to put on a condom. Once he got it on, he lay on me and spread my legs apart. Kay-Kay and I waited. I saw him moving but couldn't figure out what he was doing. We were still both waiting for him to stick it in. Finally, after about five minutes, he stopped moving.

"Damn, that was good." He said, out of breath.

"Huh?" I asked, confused. Hell, even Kay-Kay was confused. I don't remember feeling anything to this day, but we left after I pulled my pants up.

Smiling, "So can I hit it again?"

"Can you hit what again?" I asked, seriously confused.

Laughing, "You are funny."

"But I am serious. Can you hit what again?"

"Can I get it again? Seriously, you got some good pussy."

"Wait, what?"

"You got some good pussy. Can I get it again?"

"You were inside of me?"

"Stop playing, Kayla!" He said, laughing.

"Harold, I'm not joking. I didn't feel anything."

"You didn't feel me in your guts?"

Laughing, "Nigga no. All that shit you popped, don't ever pop to no chick again. And you will not come up to me and ask to hit again; I will shut you down, and you won't like my approach. If I hear on the streets that you and I were in the same bed together, the approach that I use to shut the rumor down will be worse. Got it?"

"Whatever."

"You can do whatever you want. Please take me home; I don't want to go where I was going." After that episode, I looked at whatever was going inside of me.

After that little stint, Harold would press me whenever he saw me, and I'd laugh it off. I could hear Kay-Kay say, "bitch, you better not!" After that experience, I went to summer school. I figured if I got bored, I was already in the city and could quickly get to a new dick. I went out with friends and new students on Friday night. We went to this club, and one of the new students met Harold on their own. The next day, I'm leaving my room with my other best friend, Tionne. I told her about the Harold incident the same night it happened. As we are headed to the elevator, Harold walks down the hall with the student he met the night before. He spoke to Tionne and me.

When we got to the elevator, we busted out laughing. This was in the early afternoon. Tionne and I were headed out to go shopping. When we were done, she headed home, and I returned to the dorm. When I got to my floor, Harold was waiting in the common area by the elevators. He called my name, and I stopped and spoke to him. I left when Stacy, the person he visited, came out of her room. Fifteen minutes later, Veronica came to my room and asked if I wanted to eat at the cafeteria. We were roommates during our first year and became good friends.

I did. We got our food and sat down at a table. Veronica had become friends with Stacy, so she sat at our table and began telling Veronica what had happened. She even went on to say Harold had a big dick. Gurl, I know you are fuckin lyin!!!!! That is what I said to myself, but laughing out loud was different. She asked me what was funny, and I told her that Harold having a big dick was fucking hilarious. She asked me, "How did I know?" I had to tell her what my reliable source told me. And I let her know she couldn't ask any more questions; two was her limit. I didn't tell Veronica I was the reliable source either. That was the last time Stacy spoke to me, and I didn't give a fuck. Harold saw me one weekend at home and said Stacy asked how we knew each other, and he said he told her we lived in the same town, yada yada yada yada. Oh well. She didn't have anything to worry about because I didn't want Harold, but I had to ask myself, did she like little dicks? Did she know he had a tiny dick? Or was he eating her pussy? He must be because there's no way that small dick is satisfying anybody, and if she found his dick to be big, then I must be deeeeeeeeeeeeeep...

OLD MAN

I like who I like, and I'm attracted to who I'm attracted to. If you weren't tall and athletic or just tall, I couldn't mess with you. I never messed with ugly men, men with small dicks, but never unattractive. What other females considered attractive, I never thought so. My friend Tionne kept telling me about Marion, whom she thought would be my type. I was skeptical because our taste in men was utterly different. But I went along with it. Finally, after many unsuccessful telephone attempts, I met Marion face-to-face.

One day, Tionne was going into the city, and I walked with her to the train station and waited. As we were sitting there, I noticed Marion. "Who is that standing over there?" I asked, pointing with my pinky across the street.

"That's Marion. He was the one I was telling you about." She turned to face me, "You want me to call him over here?"

"No need to; he's actually headed this way."

"Hey, Tionne, what's up? I like how you take a person's phone number and don't use it." He said as he sat down next to her.

I extended my hand in front of Tionne to shake Marion's hand. "Hi, I'm Kayla, and you would be?"

"Marion." He said as he shook my hand. "Nice to meet you. You live around here?"

"Why?" I asked.

"I've never seen you around before, that's all." "That's good, but yes, I live here."

"Well, since you two are conversing, you might as well give her your number because she's the one I got it for in the first place," Tionne said with a smile.

"I don't want your number. I want you to come up out of that fleece pullover you have on," I said, admiring it. "I need one in that color." I had many black fleece sweatshirts, but not a black Tommy Hilfiger fleece.

"Sure." He took it off and wrote down his number. "You are gonna call me, right?"

"Um, yeah." I gave Tionne the "Oh, my goodness" look as he handed me the fleece.

"Oh, look, the train is here. I gotta go. Kayla, I'll call you when I get back. Don't do anything that I would or wouldn't do." She gave me a hug and headed for the train.

"Well, it was nice meeting you, and thanks for the fleece," I said as I walked off. But before I could leave, Marion started a conversation. We talked for about two hours, getting to know each other, before spotting my cousin and getting a ride home.

I knew Marion was handsome because Kay-Kay jumped whenever I looked at him. He was about six feet five inches. Marion was basically tall, dark, and attractive. I couldn't tell if he was in shape. His clothes hid his body well, but I noticed he had a little belly when he took off the fleece, but it wasn't that bad. At least, that's what I thought. The only flaw was that he was a street pharmacist. But I kept talking to him anyway. Whenever I went into the city, Marion gave me extra money so Tionne could go. Of course, he wanted to ensure that no one tried to talk to me, but little did he know that Tionne couldn't stop me; sometimes, I couldn't stop myself. It took us about two months before I got him in bed. And when that time came.

We were at his place the first time he got inside Kay-Kay. He asked me to massage him, and I did my thing. When he turned on his back, he pulled me into him so he could kiss me. His kiss was just a kiss. He eventually made his way to my breasts. He licked, kissed, and caressed the twins. I couldn't believe that looking at him excited Kay-Kay because his mouth on the twins didn't do it all. When the twins are sucked and licked correctly, they send Kay a signal, but not this time. He finished doing whatever he was doing with the twins; he reached for a condom and put it on. I was on top, riding. Looking down at him, I realized he enjoyed it more. When he flipped me over so that he was on top...OH BOY! Remember when I said that his clothes covered his body? That's what they did. When he was on top, his belly hung. He looked like a man in his forties, but he was in his late twenties. I lay there, not wanting to touch him or for him to touch me more than he already was. "Damn, that was good," he said.

"I'm glad you enjoyed yourself." I got up and began to put on my clothes. "I have to go to work in a few hours, so I'm going home to shower and change." I kissed him on the forehead and went home. Yes, I went home mad. It was like I waited two months for nothing...DAMN!!! I felt like a dude who had been trying to fuck, and the girl got him hard, and right before he could get the condom, she changed her mind, so now he had blue balls. Dudes get mad to the point they kick a bitch out or say they're going to the store and don't return. I had never been with a man over forty, but he made it feel like I had just had sex with a perverted older man. When I got home, I stayed in the shower until I was wrinkly. While I was at work, I kept shivering and saying yuck.

Believe it or not, Marion and I dated for six months and had sex no more than five times. Each time we had sex, I would get on top, or he would hit it from behind, and after ten or fifteen minutes, he would cum, and I would be left waiting. So, during the six months we dated, I cheated a few times. The first person I cheated on him with did me so well that I couldn't walk.

Okay, so I cheated throughout the relationship with Marion. One was definitely worth it; the others were just interesting. The first time I cheated….MY GOODNESS!!!! This package was exceptional from the moment I laid eyes on him.

CAN'T WALK

When I saw Caleb, I was mesmerized. My mom was barbequing, so my brother's friend Julius would be over. It was like he could sense when my mom was barbecuing. He had become a part of the family. Julius always made me laugh, but this day was different. He brought Kay-Kay and me a gift.

Tionne and I were sitting on the deck when Julius and his two cousins came strolling around the house. "Hey, Julius, what's up?" I shouted over the balcony.

"What's going on? Where's ma and your big-headed brother at?"

"They're inside. You know how to let yourself in." I said as I couldn't take my eyes off Caleb. As my heart began to race, she started throbbing; I felt a rush. It was like all of my blood went straight to my clit. He stood about six feet four inches tall, had a medium athletic build, light skin with dreadlocks, and was sexy. He actually looked like a younger version of Bob Marley. "Please introduce us to your friends before you go in," I told Julius as I stared at Caleb.

"Oh, these are my cousins, Caleb and Davis." Then, pointing to Kayla, "That's Caden's sister and her friend Tionne." He said as he headed inside the house.

"Hello, ladies," Davis said as he sat down.

"Hey there, Davis. Caleb. Would you guys like a drink?" Kayla pointed to the tub of beverages behind Tionne, still looking at Caleb. "There's juice, soda, beer, Heinekens, and some Coronas.

"Thanks," Caleb said as he went to walk by and slightly brushed Kayla on her shoulder. "So, how are you ladies doing on this lovely day?"

"We're fine. How about you?" Tionne asked, looking at Kayla, who still couldn't take her eyes off Caleb.

"Fine." Looking at Kayla, "You have sexy, big, brown eyes," Caleb said, smiling.

"And they can't seem to take themselves off of you," Tionne said, waving her hand in front of Kayla's face.

"If you don't get your hand out of my face." She said, now looking at Tionne, then turning back to Caleb, "You're just beautiful."

"Thanks." Just then, Julius came out with a plate of food. "You went in, then there, and didn't bother to tell anybody that the food was done?"

"Ma' dukes fixed my plate. But you can go in there and make your own plates." Julius said, stuffing his mouth with potato salad as he sat at the table.

"Caleb, Davis, would you two like me to fix you a plate?" Kayla asked as she headed into the house.

"Yes, please," Caleb said with a smile. "Oh, and I don't eat pork if there is any."

"Thank you, and I eat everything," Davis said.

She went inside and fixed three plates. She would have fixed Tionne's plate, but she came behind her. They came out with the plates, and once everyone was situated, they all got their grub on.

After they were done, Julius went inside and got playing cards to play spades. The girls were partners; Julius and Davis were partners. Caleb sat between Julius and Kayla, then moved closer to her. As he rubbed her thigh, it made me wet. Afterward, they played a few hands, drank more beers, and enjoyed themselves. Finally, Kayla excused herself from the table and went to the bathroom. As she came out, Caleb pushed her back into the bathroom, closed and locked the door, and kissed her. I got to give it to her because she kissed him right back. Before they came out, Caleb ensured they wouldn't get caught. When they got back outside, plans were already made. They were all going to a party at a local club. Kayla and Tionne went inside to freshen up and met the guys in front of the house. They piled into the car and were off.

When we arrived, the whole town was at the party. When we exited the car, Caleb approached me, grabbed my hand, and headed into the club. No one knew I was in a relationship with Marion, so I had no problem having Caleb's arm wrapped around my waist. When we walked into the club, all eyes were on us. Of course, we didn't mind the stares. I found out that some of the ladies knew Caleb and had a thing for him. Julius and Davis bargained for a group rate at the door, and they succeeded. When we were inside the party, Caleb held onto me even tighter. We danced all night. I could feel that my panties were wet, which meant Kay-Kay was simmering and beginning to boil over. I was ready to fuck Caleb as soon as I saw him. With him touching me and us dancing close, she was prepared to be poked and probed. Once the party was over, everyone met up at the car, where it all began. We drove back to Julius's mother's house and sat outside. Caleb started talking to Tionne.

"Tionne, do you think Kayla would say yes if I ask her to go home with me?" He said loud enough for me to hear.

"I don't know; why don't you ask her?"

"Yes, why don't you ask me?" I said, joining their conversation.

"Well, would you come home with me this morning?" Caleb asked, smiling.

"You promise to bring me home later?"

"Are you saying yes?"

"Only if you'll take me home now so I can grab a few things."

"Goodbye, everyone," Caleb said as he grabbed Kayla's hand and walked to his car.

"Tionne needs a ride home." She said to him.

"Come on, Tionne," Caleb shouted. So they all got into the car. He dropped Tionne home, then swung by Kayla's so she could grab a few things. They then made their way to the highway. Caleb lived in Newark and sped there from Mahwah. It felt like they were on a roller coaster as fast as he was driving and hitting corners on the highway.

We finally made it to his place safely. It looked like the typical bachelor pad, nothing extravagant. He showed me around, and we finally went to his bedroom. His king-size bed was nice and comfortable. *When Kayla lay down, we felt like we were in heaven.* "Oh, I love your bed." She said, rolling around.

"I'm glad you do." He stood at the foot of the bed. "Come get up for a second." He held out his hand for me to grab. He pulled me up and gave me another kiss. Again, I didn't pull away; I kissed him right back. *By this time, I was really sweating and throbbing. He had that type of effect on me.* He took off his sneakers. He returned to the bed, lay beside me, and touched Kay-Kay.

When I felt his hand on me, I melted. I know I can't melt, but sheesh! I usually like a hand all over and inside me. You know, getting familiar with me, but Kayla still had her clothes on, which was shocking. I know he could also feel how wet I was through her clothes. Caleb moved his hands to her breasts. How dare he?! He didn't need to fuck with her breasts; I was damp and ready. All Caleb had to do was take his rod and start probing inside me. If I could have, I would have pulled off Kayla's shorts right then and there so that he could explore. Caleb caressed the twins, then removed her shirt and bra. He sucked and teased her nipples. I was pulsating, and my juices flowed as if he were already inside me. I felt like I was about to explode without him having to penetrate me. He kissed his way down to her belly button. Caleb was getting closer. I guess he was, like, he already knew Kayla, so he had to come meet me. Caleb unbuttoned her shorts and pulled both her shorts and thong off. He got up and looked at her naked body. "You have a very sexy body, Kayla. You know that?"

"Thank you," I said, smiling shyly. Caleb then proceeded to take off his clothes, and when he did. Caleb was not that hard, but hard enough, and he was perfect. His penis was the same butter complexion as his. The thickness was unbelievable. Kayla didn't think he would fit inside of me, but we would soon find out. *Before we would find out, he had to taste me. Caleb had his arms under her thighs as her legs were draped over his shoulders. He licked me like ice cream off his hands as it dripped off the cone. His tongue worshipped me as it circled around and inside me; Caleb flicked his tongue all over me. He skillfully kissed and licked my outer lips and kissed her inner thigh. Then, he returned to my outer lips and began stroking me with his tongue. Caleb kissed and licked me.*

Kayla tried to fight him off of me, but he wasn't stopping until I came. Homegirl noticed her right leg shaking; she knew what would happen. Boy, oh boy, did I explode. Caleb was now the second man to make me squirt. All Kayla could hear was him moaning and mmhmming. He kissed his way back up to her neck and her breasts. I'm sure his face was glistening from my juices. He then grabbed a condom and put it on. He teased me with the tip. His dick was so hard without using his hands, he would inch it in very slowly and take it out. I was getting pissed because I wanted it all inside of me. He started creeping it in again; the more he eased in, the wetter I got. Finally, it was all the way in. I thought that it was going to come out of Kayla's mouth, but I gripped that dick. He could only work me slowly, but I loosened up and let him work fast. He moved around in circular motions. Kayla was on her back, one leg straight and the other wrapped around his waist. He moved his body like a snake, putting his all into giving it to me. Caleb went on like that for a good twenty minutes. He put Kayla on her stomach and slightly arched her hips, and as he stroked me, my girl

Kayla was throwing me back on his shaft. The next thing I knew, she was on her side; Caleb held one leg up as he slid in and out of me. He was indeed giving it to us. Then he put her on top. He held her down on him by the hip and shoved himself inside me; Kayla didn't move. Hell, she didn't have to. I could hear Kayla gasping for air, but holding it in. Ten minutes later, we both exploded and fell asleep.

I was awakened by something rubbing against me. It was Caleb's dick. I didn't mind one bit. I also had no problem getting wet. The next thing I knew, Caleb was back inside me, pumping me slowly and in circular motions, putting his back into it. PLOT TWIST....he was in me with no condom, and it felt like heaven. In the background, Kayla's pager kept going off. It went off every ten minutes. Marion must have returned from Atlanta and was looking for her, but she wasn't going to stop what she was doing to call him back. She better not, because I don't want Caleb to stop, and I know she doesn't either, and the callback could wait. I noticed Caleb pulled out before he exploded, and before I could, I guess he saw because he came down to say hello again. As he sucked, he moved his tongue all around, and the leg started shaking again, and once Caleb realized it, he put his pretty penis back inside of me and pumped away. This time, I creamed all over his dick. Kayla got up to use the bathroom, but sat down again immediately. Kayla's legs were shaking something awful. She sat down, waited for a minute, and got back up. With her legs still shaking, she went to the bathroom and back to bed.

We went for another round, and it seemed like he spent an hour on top, hitting it from the back and side. It also seemed like Kayla spent an hour on top until we both exploded again. Kayla rode his dick in the reverse cowgirl position. He loved it when she looked back at him. Every now and again, he'd either slap her ass or tightly grab her cheeks when she was grinding on his dick. When she was dismounting from Caleb, her legs were shaking uncontrollably. We got in on for the last time before they went into the shower. Caleb had to hold Kayla up. She had never been with someone who kept her legs shaking like that. Well, at least not yet. They eventually got dressed, and Caleb took her home.

When they got in the car, she checked her pager. The pages all came from Marion. "Damn!"

"What's wrong?" He asked, rubbing her leg.

"Nothing. I forgot I had to call someone this morning."

"Well, I hope it was worth the wait." He said, smiling at her.

"My legs are still shaking, so it was worth the wait." Finally, they were turning on Kayla's street. "I had a good time yesterday, last night, this morning, and this afternoon.

"Me too. I hope that we can do this again soon. You and your brother have the same number?"

Shaking her head from side to side, "Oh hell no! We have different lines."

"Well, I hope that I get all of your numbers." He said. She went into her pocketbook, pulled out something to write her number with, and on. She handed him the paper, kissed him on the cheek, and exited the car. She had to take it step by step because her legs were still shaky.

When she got inside, she called Tionne, told her about her experience, and returned Marion's call. "Hey, how was Atlanta?"

"It was fine. Where have you been where you couldn't return my page?" He asked with an attitude.

"I've been playing volleyball all day, and there wasn't enough time between games to call you back, so I waited until I got home." She laughed to herself, being so quick with the lie.

"Oh, okay, so what are you doing now?" He asked.

"About to head into the shower." She was really going to take a bath and soak. "Why?"

"I'll be over at six. We're going out to eat and to the movies."

"Not a problem." She hung up the phone and saw it was only four, so she had enough time to soak and regroup. Marion was naturally an hour late, so they just caught a movie. As they were watching the film, Caleb paged her. She waited a few minutes before going to the 'bathroom' and calling Caleb back. Ten minutes after Marion dropped her off at home, Caleb was at her front door.

We rocked out with Caleb for the remainder of the summer. That was one of the best fucking summers, literally and figuratively. We both understood that all we were doing was fucking. Caleb KNEW I ENJOYED HIM INSIDE ME and that I had a boyfriend. Marion wanted to have sex one night after I was with Caleb. Kay-Kay would not get wet; hell, it's not that I wouldn't, I couldn't. He kept asking what was wrong; I told him I wasn't in the mood. I had a lot on my mind as I prepared to return to school. LIES!!!!! I was worn the fuck out!!!!! On to the next....

SEX WITH AN APE

Kayla was always flirting even when she didn't mean to. It just came naturally to her. Anytime she was stopped by an attractive guy on the street, she would stop and talk back. He could be a killer; it didn't matter. That was how she actually met Edwin. He pulled over and stopped in front of her. It pissed her off, but she figured, why not talk to him? He gave her his number and practically begged her to promise she would call him. She would call him only when she felt like it, like most men who gave her their numbers. He went his way, and she went hers.

Kayla and Tionne went to the local club for drinks a few days later. Who was there?

"Tionne, that's the dude I told you about the other day." She said, pointing behind the bar.

"Did you call him?" she asked curiously.

"Nope, but that doesn't mean we won't be drinking for free tonight." She said with a smile. Kayla strutted to the bar and started a conversation with Edwin. "Hey there!"

"Hey, what's up? I thought you said you were going to call me?"

"I am. I've just been so busy. I'm returning to school in a couple of weeks, so naturally, I'm shopping, packing, making rounds, and all that good stuff. Uh, can I get two Long Island Iced Teas, please?"

"Sure." He began to make drinks. "So, what year are you in? Who are these drinks for?" He asked.

"My senior year. One is for me and the other for my best friend." He placed the drinks in front of her. "How much?" She asked, reaching into her back pocket

"For you, nothing."

"Shocked, but not really. "For real?" Pretending to be shocked. "Yep, so whatever you two are drinking tonight, make sure you see me." He said with a smile.

"Thanks." *She put a few dollars in his tip jar, grabbed the drinks, and headed to Tionne, then to the dance floor. She always had a good time when she was dancing. She could just let go and be free. She would feel someone touching her ass or grinding on it occasionally. The guys who tried to talk to her when they were sober tried extra hard with assistance from alcohol. She still wasn't hearing them. She would flirt, but just enough for a drink. She eventually returned to the bar, waiting for Edwin as he had told her. While waiting, she talked with an old friend who had been trying to get with her since high school. I don't understand how men don't understand no. Edwin tapped her on the shoulder and handed her two drinks. "Thanks again." After dancing for about three hours and four Long Island Iced Teas, Kayla was done, and I was wide awake. I looked at who was heading our way. Mr. Edwin.*

"Hey, Kayla, can you wait for me?"

"Why would I wait for you?" She asked sarcastically.

"So that we can talk, and I can give you a ride home."

"What makes you think I want you to know where I live? But you know what? Tonight, I'll wait for you." She said, looking at him strangely. She went to look for her best friend, who she spotted getting her mack on. She walked over to Tionne and tapped her on the shoulder. "You alright?"

"Yeah, why?"

"Well, I'm not going home, so I want to ensure you're alright."

"Just call me when you make it home," Tionne said as she turned around to finish her conversation. "I sure will." Kayla turned, spotted Edwin, and headed toward him. They then headed over to his Land Rover and got in. "So, where are we going?"

"Well, since you won't let me take you home, how about we sit here and talk?"

"What would you like to talk about?" She asked as she settled into the seat.

"Whatever?"

"How are you gonna say you want to talk and have no idea what you want to talk about?" she asked, laughing. "So, you work with kids during the day and bartend at night?" She decided to ask to get the conversation rolling.

"Yes. I got back not too long ago from playing basketball overseas."

"Oh, really?" *We both perched up.*

"Yes, I was in Greece. So, I'll be here briefly, and hopefully, I'll be going back."

"Hopefully?" What do you mean by hopefully?"

"I enjoyed playing in Greece, but if I can't get back on the team, there's a spot open in Spain. Either way, I'll be headed somewhere." Looking around at the empty parking lot. "Do you mind if we go somewhere else?"

"Nope, not at all." He started the truck and drove out of the parking lot. He pulled into a parking lot for some apartments, which wasn't far from the club.

"Well, since you won't let me take you home, I decided to bring you to my place. Well, it's not my place, it's my dad's, and I live with him." So they got out of the car, and Kayla followed him; when they got to the door, he turned to Kayla. "You have to be very quiet."

She found it odd that a grown man was living with his dad and not the other way around. To each their own. "No problem." He opened the door, and she followed him in. He held her hand, and on the way to his room, he would turn around and give her a quiet look. They finally got to his room, and he quietly shut the door."

"Well, this is my room. Make yourself comfortable.

"Thanks." She looked around and noticed a chair at a desk. She sat in the chair. She noticed that there was no bed or air mattress. She watched him make a pallet on the floor with blankets. He walked over to his closet and returned with a shoebox when he was done. He put a towel at the bottom of the door, lit incense, and cracked open a window.

"Do you smoke?"

"Excuse me?" She was caught off guard.

"Do you smoke?" I can roll you a joint if you like."

"I'm good, thank you." As he sat there and smoked, Kayla sat beside him on his pallet and eventually lay down on her side. The blankets were extra fluffy because she couldn't tell she was lying on a hardwood floor. When he was done with his joint, he lay down.

He began kissing her neck and rubbing her side. Naturally, I made her roll over to be on her back. He played with her mini globes, which made me tingle slightly. He took off her clothes and then his. He put on a condom and came inside for a visit. He started off slow, you know, slowly getting himself inside of me, and he succeeded. Now, this is where it gets funny. As he is inside of me, he hears his father moving around. He stops, pulls out, and gets up. Yes, he actually stopped, pulled out, and got up. Her brain told me, bitch he went to the door and listened out for his father. He stood by the door like Malcolm X, peeping out the window. His father actually knocked on his door. He told him he had just gotten in and was going to bed. His dad left him alone, but why was he up at four-thirty? He came back to us and got us hot again. He came back inside of me, and man, oh man.

Edwin told Kayla to be quiet when they first entered the apartment, and now this mothafucka is loud here. His moans sounded like an ape. He had only one motion. The in and out, and that was it. He was like the Energizer bunny. He just kept going and going. The faster he went, the more he sounded like an ape, and he got louder. Finally, he was finished. I was so thankful when he went limp. He was lying on top of Kayla, and with all that weight, he probably felt like an ape.

After jamming the shit out of me, he said he was headed into the shower. As soon as he left the room, Kayla got up, quickly put her clothes on, snuck out, and got out. She ran out of the apartment building to the main street, where she could flag down a cab. Instead of going to bed, she treated me to a nice late-night/early-morning hot bath when she got home. Apparently, we both felt like we were just fucked by an ape. Hell, we could have had a better time with Mario.

CAN'T WORK IT

I was supposed to see Marion before returning to school, but he was a no-show as usual. So now I'm back at school. After I got settled in, I went for a walk around the campus. Suddenly, Kay-Kay started jumping, and I couldn't understand why until I spotted Shawn, who was headed my way. We had a class together, and he was a cutie. Nothing stood out; he was just one of those cute guys for no reason.

"Hey there." He said with a friendly smile, "Kayla, right?"

"Hey, back at you, and yes, it's Kayla. You would be?" I knew his name; I was being an asshole. "I'm Shawn. We were in the same Philosophy class last semester. I used to cheat off of you."

"So I take it you passed the class?"

"You would be right, and since you're right, I'd like to thank you."

"No need to thank me. You stay in the dorm?"

"Well, I didn't last semester, but I am this semester." Spotting a bench across the quad. "Would you like to sit down?" He asked, pointing in the direction of the bench.

"Sure, why not?" We both headed over to the bench. "So, what's your major?"

"Right now, I'm undecided. I'm thinking about Physical Therapy or Business Management. What about you?"

"Wow, it's funny you say that; I'm majoring in Physical Therapy with a minor in Business Management." I graduate this year. What year are you in?"

"My junior year, and yes, I need to decide."

Laughing, "As much as I'd like to continue this conversation, I'm hungry. So I'm gonna head back to the dorms and get something to eat."

"Is this your way of saying that I bore you?"

"I would have said that you bore me. I'm just hungry. Besides, you stay in the dorm; you can come with me unless you have a girlfriend or stalker and don't want to be seen with me."

"It's not even like that." He said with his cute smile. Shawn was exactly six feet tall. Caramel complexion with hazel eyes. He had a small oval head and a low haircut, but today he wore a baseball cap. He had very little facial hair. He was in great shape; I could see his abs peeking through his tank top. I also must admit he was sexy and cute. If that's a type. As we walked away, I accidentally dropped my keys to get a peek at his ass. "Do you like what you see?"

"Excuse me?" I couldn't believe that I got caught.

"I can feel you looking at my ass. Is it okay?" He asked as he poked it out and turned around.

"I have no idea what you're talking about. I dropped my keys and picked them up. Just because you can feel me looking at your ass doesn't mean I'm looking at it, but you have a nice ass." I said, trying not to laugh.

"Whatever. So, do you have a roommate or a single room?"

"I'm an R.A., so I have my own room. What about you?"

"I have a roommate, and we stay on the floor with apartments."

"Great, can I come by and cook something to eat?" I asked jokingly. "My bad; I can cook enough for you and your roommate." I opened the door to the dorm lobby, and he followed behind. We headed to the cafeteria and decided on sandwiches. We grabbed some chips and something to drink when they were done making our sandwiches. We swiped our ID cards and found a booth to sit in.

"Yeah, you can make something for you and me to eat." He said with a smile.

"So this is your junior year?" I changed the topic before it went somewhere I didn't want it to.

"Yep, one more to go, and I'm done. Hopefully. Gotta figure the major thing out." "Yeah, that would help determine whether you have another year left. So, did you commute for the first two years? What made you decide to stay on campus?"

"I did. The commute from Long Island was a little too much, along with trying to work. But I saved enough money to pay for the dorms, so I don't have to over-exhaust myself. What made you decide to become an R.A.?"

"My R.A. from last year suggested that I apply. So I did and got it."

"Cool, so uh, do you have a man? If so, on or off-campus?" He asked before taking a bite of his sandwich

"Ah, I have a man who lives forty-five minutes away. Why do you ask?"

"You are too pretty to be single unless you're crazy, and I wouldn't believe you if you said you didn't have a man. Does the distance bother you?"

"Even when we're five minutes away, it's still like we are forty-five minutes away. Sometimes, I don't even know why we're still together. And I can still be crazy and have a man. I know how to control my craziness." I said before taking a sip of juice.

"Have you ever cheated on him? And did you say you know how to control your craziness?"

Without hesitation, "All summer long. And yes, I did. I have my craziness under tight wraps."

Amazed, "Would you do it again?"

Laughing, "Yes."

"What?! So why are you with him?"

"Honestly, I keep asking myself that same question. At first, it was good, but after we had sex for the first time, I lost interest. But on top of that, Marion's not a man of his word. He'll say one thing and do the opposite. I could have been another notch in his belt, cause I know he damn sure wasn't another notch in my belt. Shit, I don't even wear belts. We don't have anything in common. Maybe it was for shits and giggles, more shits than giggles. I don't know."

"Does he work or go to school?"

"He's a street pharmacist, and his hours are from three to midnight. The only thing he was suitable for was money. Sex isn't that good; hence, the reason I lost interest."

"Again, so why are you with him?"

"I honestly don't know. I thought it would be a summer fling, but we are still together."

"I guess I'm asking, why be with someone who wants to be with you for convenience? Why not leave?"

"I honestly don't know." Eating my last chip. "Well, as much as I'd love to finish this conversation, I still have my computer to hook up. You can come by; I'm on the ninth floor." I gathered my things and went to my room. When I got to my room, my phone was ringing. "Hello."

"Hey, sweetheart, how are you?" It was Marion.

"I'm fine, and you?"

"Good. Where are you?"

"I'm back at school. I told you yesterday morning that I was leaving this morning, and you said you would be over last night, but we know how you do."

"What's that supposed to mean?"

"It means I wanted to see you last night, and naturally, you didn't show up without calling."

"Money calls."

"Whatever. I still have things to do, so I have to go." I hung up and began hooking up my computer and printer. Once I was done, I sat down to relax; a knock was at my door. "Who is it?"

"Shawn."

I got up to open the door, "Hey, come on in."

"I hope this is not too soon." He said, laughing.

Laughing, "With your jacket? Uh, no, not too soon."

"Oh yeah, my jacket, I was on my way to the store, and I thought I could get you to walk with me."

"Sure, why not?" I grabbed my jacket and some money, and we headed to the bodega a few blocks away. He got a six-pack of Coronas, I got a few bottles of Snapple, and we returned to the dorms. We got comfortable when we returned to my room and downed the Coronas in less than an hour.

"Kayla."

"Yes?"

"Can I kiss you?"

"Wha." Before I could get it out, he kissed me. It was a nice kiss. He made Kay-Kay jump and wet at the same time. The next thing I knew, he was feeling all over her.

"Oh, you are wet."

"Well, that happens when I get turned on, "I laughed.

"Oh, and she's fat."

"Is that a good thing or a bad thing?"

"That's a good thing." He pretty much ripped off my clothes and went down and kissed Kay-Kay. He kept it friendly and straightforward with his tongue inside of her. He would switch his tongue movements every now and then. His tongue would move back and forth, or he would solidify it as I fucked his face. Once he felt my leg beginning to shake, he whipped it out. MY MOUTH DROPPED when I saw what was about to go inside me. He was hard, more than twelve inches long, and thick. I had to take a deep breath. He slowly inserted himself inside of Kay-Kay. In and out he went. It felt like I was with Ediwn again, in and out, in and out. Kay-Kay would tighten up occasionally, but it wasn't like it mattered. I started looking around the room.

Yes, I was bored, and he wasn't doing it for Kay-Kay or me. I took another deep breath and flipped him over to be on top. I began to grind on him because there was no way I was going up and down on that long blade. Grinding was best because I didn't want to tear my insides up. Kay-Kay and I did our thing. He came, and I orgasmed. "Oh, you got some good shit." Oh no, he didn't call her shit. He could have said pussy, but he chose shit. Her name is Kay-Kay. What do you expect from a guy with a BIG DICK who doesn't know how to use it?

"Thanks, and her name is Kay-Kay. Not shit."

"You know what I mean." He said as he played with Kay-Kay's little bit of hair. "So you think we could do this again?"

"Huh?" I heard him, but wanted him to repeat himself.

"Could we do this again?"

"Nah, I'm good." Did I say that?

"What do you mean, you good?"

"What we did just wasn't worth a second time."

"That's messed up." He said, shaking his head.

"It wasn't meant to sound messed up; it's just the truth. What is messed up is that you have a BIG DICK and don't know how to use it properly. Don't get me wrong, you're a nice person, and we can still be friends, but as far as us having sex again, that's not happening. Oh, and don't worry, your secret is safe with me."

"I don't know if I should be mad or offended?"

"Neither. Why be mad? Be grateful that I'm being honest with you."

"I've had females tell me it's too big and it hurts, but not I don't know what I'm doing with it."

"Yeah, they have been telling you it hurts. That's another way of saying you're not doing something right. I'ma tell it like it is."

"Well, I respect that, and I wouldn't mind having a REAL friend."

"Well, on that note, I'm headed for the shower. If you are here when I get out, cool; if not, no love is lost." Before I showered, I grabbed a can with a few pre-rolled blunts. I lit the incense that I had in there as well. I heard my door shut; I peeped and saw Shawn was gone. Thank goodness. I came out, lit more incense in my room, and opened all the windows.

I lit my blunt and began to puff away. I know I can be rude sometimes, but do I care? No, not really. "Oh shit!" I said to myself as I was smoking. It hit me that this was the same dude who convinced Veronica that she wasn't bisexual but really gay. I started laughing and couldn't stop. I remember her telling me about her first sexual experience with a guy. I remember her telling me that it was painful. She described Shawn to the T, including his dick and motion. She said it was so unbearable that she didn't want to experience anything like that again, so she turned entirely to the ladies and never looked back, which was three years ago. When she told me I was high as a kite, I couldn't stop laughing then, and I can't stop laughing now. In the few years I've known her, I've always said she needs some good dick, and she always said no, pussy and a dildo were good enough. Now I understand why she says that. Shawn traumatized her.

As I sit here and smoke, I think about how Veronica and her friend Vicki had a bet. You'd think she was a guy if you didn't hear Vicki speak. On the short side, Vicki kept her hair cut low and rocked a baseball cap when her hair wasn't done. She was very much butch. Ronnie, on the other hand, was a girly tomboy. She loved to have her hair and nails done. The bet was to see how many girls they could bag or sleep with. They were talking about a bet in front of me.

In my head, I was like, these two mothafuckas are just like dudes. They were asking each other how many they had. When they said how much they had, they paused after stating their numbers, looked at me, and said, "a half." Vickie said two and a half, and Ronnie said she had three and a half. No bitches ya'll are at two and three. I'm nobody's half, and ya'll ain't slick. I love dick way too much. Ronnie was known for turning chicks out, but I wasn't the one who either one was turning out. Vicki was so sweet and caring; I tutored her in Spanish and got to know her. Those two were my girls. I loved them both to death, but it wasn't going down. I remember one night after a party, Ronnie was in my room, and we talked. She asked me why I had never kissed her. First, I'm not into girls, and second, why would I want to kiss her? To say I kissed a girl? Yeah, I kissed her. Ronnie turned out a girl I had been friends with since our first year here. She told me after it happened. Her name was Diane. The day after it happened, she said, Kay, I need to talk to you. I told her to come to my room. She came with weed. When she came to my room, she was nervous. I asked her what was wrong, and she said my name as if she were stressed. She was shaking as she rolled the blunt. I took it away and told her to talk as I rolled up. I returned it when I was done because she needed to smoke more than I did. She said she needed to hit the blunt before she said anything. She did, and as she was exhaling, she told me she let Veronica eat her out. I was shocked. She continued telling me they were in her room, that she was smoking, and that she went to lie on the bed, and Veronica lay beside her. She said they were talking, and the next thing she said, Ronnie was between her legs, and she didn't stop her.

I also asked her if she would let her do it again; she would, and she did. She said she wasn't gay, and the crazy thing was she was a Rastafarian, and her parents would kill her if they found out, but Ronnie was good at eating pussy. It was a lot to take in at the moment, but they were both my friends, so whatever made them happy or whatever they were going to do, then hey. After that semester, Diane didn't return to school. Ronnie won the bet between her and Vicki four to three. I must say that Vicki pulled some bad bitches; they had natural BBLs. Ronnie, too, but Vicki's chicks were banging. Her chicks had guys asking her if they had straight or bisexual friends who looked like them. After finishing my blunt, I went to shower and bed. I hate getting high sometimes. I am thinking about shit that happened in the past and then linking two things that have nothing to do with each other. Oh well

CONDOM BROKE

After my last class, I had to hurry to my room to freshen up and prepare for a go-see. I walked in a few fashion shows and occasionally did some catalog work. I wasn't that serious about modeling; it was just something to do for extra cash. I went to my go-see, and by the time I got back to my room, there was a message letting me know I had gotten the job. The job was for a fashion show, which meant I would be well paid. I was so in a hurry to change into a pair of sweatpants and wash the makeup off my face that I forgot to pick up my mail, so I headed back downstairs to the mailboxes.

While in the lobby, I stopped to talk to Veronica and met some new students. I have to give it myself; I don't care how others perceive me, knowing I'm far from arrogant yet secure with who I am. Those who don't know me will think I'm vain, and those who know me will tell you it's all confidence. I say that because I saw some of the new girls trying to kick it to a few basketball players, and when I said hello to the guys, I got a few evil eyes. The players stopped talking to them to say hello and asked how I was doing. I also noticed that a few new girls had stayed on my floor, and I made sure they heard what I had to say. "I hope you basketball players don't make me come after ya'll. If my girls tell me you did something to them, I'm gonna hurt ya'll." I looked at the young ladies, winked, and gave them a friendly smile. "You girls, be safe; you know where I am if you need me."

"Hey, Kayla, what's up?" I heard someone shout out to me. When I turned around, it was Shawn.

"Hey, what's going on?" "I need a favor. I need help in a class."

"Which one?" I asked curiously.

"Vicki told me you tutored her in Spanish last year, and she got an A, so I was wondering if you could help me?"

My godfather was Spanish and taught me by speaking to me in Spanish. Spanish eventually became my second language. I breezed through learning Spanish in junior high and high school. All my Spanish teachers thought I was Spanish because I was so fluent and able to converse. My godfather knew what he was doing. And my parents didn't object. "Sure. When do you have Spanish class?"

"Tuesdays and Thursdays at five."

"Well, I can help. Let me know when you want the help, and you can come to my room, or I can come down to yours. Just let me know."

He kissed me on the cheek, "Thanks."

"No problem." I turned back and headed towards the elevators, where I spotted Dick. No, not a dick but Dick, as in Richard, who was about six foot six; of course, he had an athletic build, very muscular. He had a little mustache and a close haircut, and his head was shaped like Stewie's from Family Guy. He had tired, brown eyes. He was heavily recruited and was now the star basketball player. We've spoken and even had a class together in our first and second years. All the girls loved him; I wasn't that impressed.

"Hi, Miss Kayla; how are you?" He said politely.

"I'm fine, and you?" "I'm doing well. Since I've been here, I haven't seen you; where have you been?"

"Uh, let's see, there's class, then I work every now and then, and now I'm an R.A., so I've been on my floor a lot getting to know my girls. But now, since everything is in order, I guess you'll see me hanging out more."

"What floor?" He asked when the elevator doors opened, and we entered.

"The ninth floor, thank you." I noticed he pushed the button for the seventh floor.

"I'm in seven C." He said with a big smile.

"Okay, thanks," I said sarcastically. "Oh well, this is your floor," I said as the doors opened.

"Well, I'll see you later." He said as he was walking off the elevator. Finally, the doors closed, and I could only shake my head. When I got to my floor, a group of girls stood by my door. "How can I help you, ladies?"

"Hi, Kayla, we just wanted to talk," Nicole said.

I opened my door, and they followed me in. "Have a seat." Walking into my room, I had my double bed against the right wall with a small entertainment center across from it. My couch was to the right of my bed. There was a table in the corner with four chairs to the left of my couch. It's not too far from the entertainment center. My desk was on the left side of my bed, next to the bathroom door. I had a purple throw rug in the center of my room that matched my linens. I had just finally completed my room. The girls sat at the table, and I sat on the couch. "So, what's on your mind, ladies?"

"How do you do it?" Nicole asked

"How do I do what?"

"Remain so calm around those guys?" Michelle asked. Nicole and Michelle were roommates, and this was their first year. I liked them because, in a way, they reminded me of Tionne and me. They had been best friends since they were five and did everything together. They somehow automatically became my favorites.

"I don't know. Since I already know everybody, it's easy for me. But at the same time, we all started here the same year, and we've become friends. Living in a dorm like this, everyone becomes friends and family."

"What was your first year like here?" Michelle asked.

"Well, my first year was easy, at least to me. I took summer classes, so the basketball team was the first group of people I met. I also met my roommate, and we hung out a lot. Once school started, I adjusted. It was pretty much party central. You have to know when and when not to party. I studied, worked, and then partied. So many girls came in, partied, studied, and are no longer here. I don't want to come off as sounding like a parent, but I want ya'll to get your priorities straight. If you ever need help with anything, don't hesitate to contact me. I will scold you like a big sister, but I have your back, right or wrong."

"You're like a big sister already," Nicole said with a smile. "And that's a good thing. Thanks."

"Yeah, what she said."

"Not a problem." The girls got up and left. I went into the bathroom, washed my face, brushed my teeth, and showered. When I got out, I put some lotion on, put on my robe, and lay down. Five minutes later, I heard a knock at my door. "Who is it?" I asked as I headed towards the door.

"Dick."

I was surprised. Dick was on the other side of the door. "Come in."

He came in and sat down on the couch. "Can I talk to you?"

"Sure, what's up?"

He looked around the room. "The way you have it set up is really nice."

"Thank you. It took me a minute, but I got it the way I wanted."

"You're welcome. Did anyone help you?"

"My mom did my bathroom, and I did everything else."

"Cool." Looking at my pictures, "Who are these in the pictures?"

"My family. Why are you asking me so many damn questions?" I asked as I went into the bathroom to put on my pajamas.

When I came out, Dick kissed me at the door. He put on my Joe CD, carried me to the bed, and kissed my neck. He took his time caressing the twins. It was like I was in heaven, but then again, I'd been here. He licked, sucked, and lightly bit on my nipples. He was doing a pretty damn good job because that tingle went down my spine and woke Kay-Kay up. He went down and introduced himself to Kay-Kay. He kissed her the way he kissed me. Although it was a nice kiss, my legs didn't shake. He then pulled off his pants, and before throwing them on the floor, he grabbed the condom out of his pocket. It was dark, but the light from the outside was enough. He was hard, but his dick was short and fat. And I mean Vienna sausage short. Now, what was that going to do? Why didn't I stop him at the kiss? When he went in, he came right back out. It lasted all of two minutes. He went in, exploded, and that was it.

"The condom broke." He said.

'What? The condom, what? Get up off me." I said, rushing to the bathroom. I grabbed the mirror out of the medicine cabinet, turned on the hot water, and then put one leg on the sink to see any traces of cum. I was ready to try wiping it out with a hot rag if there were any. I saw nothing.

"I don't have any more condoms, do you?" He asked as I was coming out of the bathroom.

"Nope." I was lying. I had a drawer full of them.

"Well, could I come back tomorrow, and we can finish?" He asked, putting on his clothes.

"Call me," I said as I walked him to the door. He tried to kiss me on the cheek, but I stepped back and closed the door. He must be crazy if I let him get another try at Kay-Kay. The condom broke, yeah, okay. Something made me walk over to the garbage to see if he had put it there. There was a condom. I grabbed a tissue, got it out, and looked at it. Just as I thought. The condom didn't break and was full of cum. He was just a two-minute man.

It was Halloween when Marion decided to visit me at school. When he got there, everything was fantastic. We talked and joked around. Afterward, he fell asleep as I was lying there watching television. When I heard him snore, I dressed and went to Veronica's room to smoke. I stayed there for a while. When I finally returned to my room, Marion was still asleep; at least, I thought he was.

The following day, when we woke up, he went into the bathroom. He was in there too long, and I had to use the bathroom, so I went to the bathroom on my floor. When I returned to the room and stepped away from the door, a cup with water fell. He had put the cup on the hinge so it would fall on my head. Apparently, when I left the room the night before, he got up and did some snooping. He found some money in a card that was inside my desk drawer. Not on top but inside. Derrick surprised me earlier by stopping by. I signed him out just as Marion walked to the dorm door. As soon as I let go of Derrick's hug and he turned to walk out, Marion was walking in. Marion didn't know Derrick, but Derrick knew who he was.

Anyway, the night before, I had a date with my father. We went to a play and dinner. Before he left, he gave me some money. Derick's sole purpose for visiting me was because my birthday was in two days. So he brought me my birthday card with cash; I added the money from my dad and stuck it inside the card. So, he assumed Derrick gave me the money, and I let him run with that. He then brought up that I had left him alone in the room. Then the motherfucker hit me. That's when he had to go. We argued all the way to the lobby. I knew his ID wouldn't be there because I wasn't the RA on duty and didn't have an overnight pass for him. So I knew we had to go to the security office. On our way there, he's still talking shit, and I tell him to be quiet so I can get his ID. Did he listen? No. The guards asked me if I was alright, and I told them I was. But, here goes this mothafucka again, now beefing with the security guards who were ready to fight him. Finally, I got the okay to leave from one of the security guards, and I did that.

I went back to the dorm. I was going to go to Veronica's room, but then I saw Chad, my friend with benefits. He and I had been fucking since we were freshmen. We were each other's little secret.

Quick Side Bar -One night, we had a party in the dorm on all floors; Chad got so drunk that he passed out, and I couldn't wake him up for shit…I was so fucking horny. His roommate constantly flirted with me and was the one who set us up, so I was like fuck it. With Chad passed out in his bed, I fucked his roommate. If Chad ever found out, he said nothing to me because we did fuck the next day…

So, I ended up having breakfast with him. He asked me whether I had heard the couple arguing outside. I told him that it was me. After breakfast, I headed to my room; my phone rang as soon as I arrived. It was the guard on duty. Marion was down there.

I went back down and walked him to his car. I remember him picking me up and attempting to throw me at a car coming our way. I held on tight to his neck. The car passed, and he put me down and left.

I returned to the dorm, thinking he was crazy, and that we could break up now. Especially after he hit me. When he got home, he told his mother that the security guard said they'd mail his ID rather than give it back to him. Had he just shut the fuck up, he could have gotten it. His mother called and asked what happened; he left out the part where he hit me. She asked me if I wanted to speak to him. NOPE!!!! After that, we didn't talk until Thanksgiving; my birthday was two days after the incident. Wait, he called me on my birthday but asked if I missed him —nope. Never said happy birthday or even called back to say it.

And to think, I used to go into the city with his cousin and pick up their product. Yes, I would hide his shit in my bra under my tit, and we'd keep it moving until we got back home. I was a ride-or-die chick for this ass. Damn, I was stupid.

Between Shawn and Dick, I was done with fucking any guys in the dorm. Well, that's what I told myself, and I believed that. About a week after that incident with Marion, I was horny, so I fucked my one friend with benefits, Chad. He wasn't that good, but he wasn't that bad. He'd get me there, but could never make me orgasm. I'd have to go to my room and rub one out. I actually introduced him to Marion. He knew who Marion was, but Marion didn't have the slightest clue who Chad was or that I was fucking him. Chad got on the elevator and headed to do his laundry when I signed Derrick out. When I was done signing Marion in, we got on the elevator, and what do you know, there was Chad. We both laughed; he shook his head. Chad also knew Derrick was my ex. After I gained my composure, I introduced them cause I had started a conversation with Chad. When Chad got off on his floor, Marion asked me if I was fucking him. Currently, occasionally, but he didn't have to know that. Years later, I told him the truth when we weren't together....Oh well!

UNCIRCUMCISED

Marion finally called me at my mother's on Thanksgiving Day. "Kayla, pick up the phone." My mom shouted.

"Hello."

"Hey, sweetie, how are you?"

I knew it was Marion just by the Hey, sweetie. "Fine, and you?"

"Can I see you tonight?" "If you want to. Just page me to make sure that I am around." I said casually.

That pissed him off. "What do you mean, page you?"

"You know how you like to do. I'm not waiting around for you to come and not show. So when you're ready to see me, page me." I hung up the phone and picked up my conversation with Tionne, sitting beside me on the couch, laughing. "If he thinks I'm going to sit around waiting for him, he's got another thing coming."

"It's not like you did it before," Tionne laughed.

"True. Marion said he's coming over later; we shall see." Tionne and I ate again and watched some football. About an hour later, my pager went off; it was Marion. I waited 45 minutes before calling him back. He said he was on his way. When he got to the house, he beeped his horn. "If you hear me scream or any noise from outside, call

The cops," I told Tionne before heading outside. I could see him smiling from the front door.

"Hey, Kayla, how are you?" He asked as I got into the car.

Very short. "Fine."

"I've missed you." He said, stroking the side of my face.

"Really?" I asked, moving my face away.

"So, how's school? When's the last time you had sex?"

He would always ask me that, and I'd give him the later date that we had sex, but not this time. "School's great; I passed all my mid-terms, and the last time I had sex was a few days ago."

"I didn't see you a few days ago."

"You asked me the last time I had sex, and I told you." I could see his face drop out of the corner of my eyes. "You know, Marion, this relationship isn't working for me. When I give myself to someone, that's what I do. I may get busy, but I always make time. If I can't do something, I will always let you know. I've never left you hanging, and that's what you do. If you say you're coming over, you don't, and you don't even have the decency to call and say so. I'm so tired. I'm starting to get migraines, not headaches but fucking migraines. Your partner isn't supposed to make you sick; you make me sick, literally and figuratively. I can't do this. You make me sick, and I mean that.

"Damn." He said with his head still hanging down.

"It was what it was." I opened the door. "Oh, and by the way, this wasn't the first time I cheated on you either." I got out of the car and went back inside the house. Tionne and I heard his car start and drive off a half-hour later. When I looked out the window, Marion was driving off.

A few hours after seeing Marion, I got a page from Darron, a guy I had a class with. He asked me for my pager number on the last day of class before our Thanksgiving break. He thought we could hang out. I gave him my pager number without thinking about why he asked for it. It surprised me when I saw his number on my pager; I honestly didn't believe he would page me. I was actually glad that he paged me. I gave him a callback. "Hello, may I speak to Darron?"

"Speaking."

"Hey, what's up? It's Kayla."

"I'm good; how are you?" He then got straight to the point, "What are you doing tomorrow?"

It was Black Friday, and I wasn't trying to get out in crowds. "Nothing. Why?" I asked curiously. "I was wondering if you could come to see me. Any time is good."

"Well, I can do that. Does three sound good?"

"Yes, and you remember how to get to my house?"

"Yes, I do." I had to think for a minute since it was back in September that we had a study group at his house. "Yeah, I remember how to get there. If not, I can always call you."

"So I'll see you tomorrow around three." He hung up.

I went to bed and got up early the following morning. I did what I had to do around the house for my mom and then got ready to see Darron. I had Tionne go with me to the train station. While we were there, we saw Marion. He approached us and started a conversation as if nothing had happened the night before.

"Hey, Kayla and Tionne."

Tionne responded, "Hey there, Marion."

"I can't stay and talk to you guys because I'm waiting for a friend."

"Nobody asked you to come over here, and nobody cares why you're here," I said sarcastically, but I meant what I said.

"It's like that?" He asked.

"Yep." I turned back to Tionne to finish our conversation.

"Well, I guess I'm going to leave." He said, but we weren't paying him any attention. "I said I'm leaving." He repeated himself.

"We heard you the first time," I said as I realized my train had just pulled in. I gathered my things. "Tionne, I'll call you when I get back or if I decide to go back to the dorm." I got on the train and headed to see Darron.

When I arrived at the train station, he was waiting for me. He greeted me with a hug. Then, we headed to his house. When we got there, he allowed me to get comfortable. Since we had a biology class together, we sat beside each other. So we pretty much knew each other. As we enjoyed music, each other's company, and the little conversation about nothing, we lay there holding each other, rubbing each other's backs. His head was on my shoulder, and he traced my breasts over my shirt. He eventually made his way underneath my shirt. He made Kay-Kay tingle. He took off my shirt and explored my upper body.

He nibbled on my ears, kissed me on the neck, and gave me one of the most passionate kisses. Then, he pulled off his shirt, and I kissed him on the neck and nibbled on his ear. Then, he took my pants off, placed my thong to the side, and tasted Kay-Kay. "Mmm." He said as he licked her. "You taste good."

"Thank you." His strokes were deep. When he licked her, he made sure that he licked her. With his tongue, he wrote the alphabet inside Kay-Kay. Then, he coiled his tongue inside of her. He was able to move his tongue like a snake while in Kay-Kay. A trick he was always showing me in class. Whenever he did that, Kay-Kay would get wet. Now, he was inside Kay-Kay....Oh my!!!!! "Oh, Darron, that feels good." I moaned. He kept at it until he felt my body starting to shake. This time was different, though. He was so good orally that I thought my entire body was numb, including Kay-Kay. Fifteen minutes later, Kay-Kay exploded, and my legs began to shake. Darron got me to an s orgasm, better known as a squirting orgasm. Then he pulled his dick out. He wasn't circumcised; Darron had that extra skin to pull back before putting on the condom. Why wasn't he circumcised?! This was the first for me, but when the foreskin was pulled back, what a pretty penis it was. Next, he placed himself inside of Kay-Kay. His movements were so right. He started slow but never got that fast; it was like he was making love to Kay-Kay and me. As he pumped, Kay-Kay flexed her muscles. She tightened herself around his penis, making it hard for him to escape her. He placed one of my legs over his shoulder, and the other wrapped around his waist as he thrust Kay-Kay. He flipped me over, arched my hips, spread my legs apart, and slowly hit me from the back. Next, he closed my legs while still inside me, making me lie on my stomach.

As his legs were outside mine, he pumped and continued to work us slowly. He made me get on my side after a few minutes in the position. He held my top leg as he entered behind me and then rested my leg on him. He played with my breasts as he hit Kay-Kay and got back on top. After Kay-Kay creamed, he did the ultimate. He went face-to-face with Kay-Kay again. He started to suck and lick on her. He stopped. "When I'm feeling somebody, I do it before and after." He said.

Smiling, "Well, I guess you are feeling me."

"Oh, yes." He went back to licking and sucking Kay-Kay until she exploded again. He stopped. "Okay, Ms. Squirter." His face was glazed. We lay there for a minute before falling asleep, and when I woke up, I showered, dressed, and headed home.

When I arrived at the train station at home, I saw Marion and hoped and prayed that he didn't see me. "Kayla!" He shouted.

"Damn!" I turned away and kept walking, pretending not to hear him. But he caught up to me.

"Where are you coming from?" He asked.

"Minding my business."

"Oh, it's like that?"

"Yes, it is. We are no longer a couple, and I don't need to tell you where I'm going or coming from."

"Well, I guess I'll see you around." He said as if it was going to bother me.

"Whatever." I got into a cab and headed home. When I got there, I crashed into my bed in my clothes. It was Sunday morning when I woke up; I slept through Saturday, and nobody bothered to check on me. Darron honestly wore my ass out. I could still run a few errands before my mom took me back to school.

When I returned to the dorms, I got situated, put my goodies away, visited with my girls, and got ready for the week. I spoke to Darron and went to bed. When we were in class, everything was still everything. I invited him to come home with me on the weekend coming up. He did.

We got a little freaky on the train ride home. We had our jackets wrapped around us. Darron played with the twins, and I had his dick in my hand. As I stroked him, he began to get hard. Darron stuck his hand inside my pants and inside Kay-Kay. I don't know how we both did it, but I managed to make him cum, and he made me orgasm. I must admit it was a lovely train ride home. When we got to the house, I introduced him to my mother. I showed him to the guest bedroom, then to mine. After dinner, my mother left. Then, I jumped into the shower in my mother's bedroom while he showered in the main bathroom.

When my mother returned, we watched a movie in the family room. After the movie, she went to her bedroom and fell asleep. When I heard her snoring, Darron and I finished what we had started on the train. First, I straddled Darron and kissed his neck as he sucked on my breasts. Kay-Kay felt it when he was hard. Next, he moved my shorts to the side. ANOTHER PLOT TWIST… without a condom, he entered as I was still on top of him. He held on tight to my hips. He actually moved me up and down, and it felt good. He then flipped me onto my back. He had one of my legs hanging over the back of the couch and the other wrapped around his waist as he embedded his dick inside me until we both came.

I felt him taking off my shorts as I lay on the couch. He was face-to-face with Kay-Kay and began his tongue-twisting, alphabet spelling thing with his tongue. When she creamed, he made sure to taste everything and that she was dry.

He was up early the following day, as was my mother. When he entered my room, he woke me up by waking Kay-Kay. He was just so good at tasting her. I tried to move his head from between my legs, but wasn't successful. He finally stopped when she squirted. "Damn, you taste good."

"Now, that is a nice way to wake up. Is my mother here?"

As he was pulling out his rock-hard dick. "Nope. She said she'll be back in an hour." So he said as he opened my legs and placed himself inside her. This time, he really hit me off. Instead of going slowly, he kept a steady pace. First, he had my legs spread over his shoulders. He used his hands to balance himself. Then he held onto my headboard as he worked me; it felt so good. He then got me out of bed and made me bend over. My hands were on the bed. And he entered Kay-Kay from behind, holding onto my hips; it sounded like macaroni and cheese being stirred. That's the best way to describe how wet I was; he was still going. The next orgasm I had was a multiple orgasm. When we finished and cleaned up, my mother came home. Darron and I went out, and dinner was ready when we returned. We ate with my mother, went to the movies, returned to an empty house, and got comfortable. He stood before me and squatted as I was lying on the couch. Then, He pulled my pants off and stuck his tongue inside Kay-Kay. Then, he spelled my name, went through the alphabet forwards, backward, and from the middle. When he was done, he left me trembling in a wet spot on the couch and went to bed.

We returned to my dorm room the following day and then to his house. He stayed in Kay-Kay all night. Eventually, we went to sleep, but when I woke up the next day, I was awakened by him playing with Kay-Kay with the tip of his penis. I guess he pulled the skin back before I could wake up. Then, he stuck it in and worked us good. Every time he got inside me, he ensured Kay-Kay had multiple orgasms. It was all about her; I was just there for the ride.

Darron and I actually dated for a semester. Well, we were in a situationship. We weren't a couple, but we spent much time together and fucked during that time. So maybe you can say we were just fuck buddies. I must say that, at times, his actions were those of a boyfriend. I had one male friend, Nick, with whom I was really cool with, which bothered him. Whenever he and I walked on campus and Nick called out my name, I'd tell Darron to hold on and see what Nick wanted. Or if we were in the student lounge and he was ready to go, and I was talking to Nick, I wouldn't leave until we finished our conversation. I'd give him the key to my room so he could wait. He didn't like that.

I didn't see anything wrong; Nick was just my friend, nothing more. Right before Winter Break, we were all at the campus lounge drinking and getting carried away. I kissed someone, and I honestly didn't think twice about it. Darron heard about it. By the time I got home, my pager was going off. When I finally called him back, he was pissed. I tried to deny it, saying it wasn't a real kiss; it only looked like one because I was sitting on his lap. Then I heard myself and was like bitch shut the fuck up now.

Eventually, I got him to calm down, and we made nice over the phone, but I knew it was a massive strike against me. A few weeks later, Nick caught me in the lounge; I was waiting for Darron to get out of class; he was spending the night. Nick offered to buy me a beer because he needed to talk to me. I accepted his offer. He said, "Take this information and do what you want with it." In my head, I'm like, this can't be good. He tells me that Darron has a girlfriend and that they are still together.

Nick was walking behind her and her friend and overheard the conversation. They had never broken up. I asked him if he was sure it was her, and he said yes because she greeted him when he came out of class with more than a kiss on the cheek. He walked her to class, which was across from his. The class I was waiting for him to finish. I looked at the time, guzzled my beer, and decided to wait for him by the class. I got there at the perfect time. I approached them and asked if he was still spending the night. She looked at me like I was crazy. I turned to Darron and asked him if she was his girlfriend. She chimed in and answered for him. She said yes. I turned and told her that's not what he told me. I turned back to him and told him he was worried about who I was kissing and that he had a whole girlfriend. I shook my head and walked off. He did come after me, and I told him he could have been honest. Was this another lesson learned? Nope, not at all. I just moved on to the next...Could this be karma? Who the fuck knows? But damn, he didn't have to put it on me like that with his magnificent tongue skills and uncircumcised dick.

LENNY KRAVITZ

It didn't take me long to get over Darron. When I'm not doing anything, you can often find me chatting online, meeting new people, and getting free meals. One night, in particular, I was online chatting away when I received an instant message from someone I knew, Jack. After we chatted for a while, he gave me his phone number. After finishing my other conversations, I called him. "Hey Jack, what's going on?"

"Nothing, sitting here chilling out listening to some Lenny."

"Lenny Williams or Lenny Kravitz?" Lenny Williams is old school — someone my mom would listen to — but why would I call out his name? I don't know.

"Lenny Kravitz." He said, holding in his laugh. "Why in the hell would I be listening to Lenny Williams? I'm twenty-five, not fifty-five."

"My bad. I love Lenny Kravitz."

"You listen to Lenny Kravitz?" He asked, shocked. "I love his music."

"When it comes to music, I'm a bit versatile. Whenever I play Lenny Kravitz's music, people look at me crazy."

"He's the shit."

"That he is. By chance, do you have his first album? I lost it, and I've had difficulty finding it."

"Yes, I do. Would you like to borrow it?"

"Now, if I didn't want to borrow it or tell you about my trouble finding it, I wouldn't have asked you if you had it now, would I?"

"That's what I like about you." I could tell he was smiling.

"And what's that?"

"Your sarcasm. It turns me on so much."

"Does it really?" I had known Jack for about five years. He moved next door to my grandmother, and anytime I'd visit her, he'd always be outside on his stoop talking to his friends. I thought he was mixed, half white and half black, but nope, entirely black, just light-skinned with dreadlocks, just like Lenny. He was of medium build. He didn't work out, but he was in shape. In some odd way, I found myself attracted, sexually-that is, to him. And with that, I decided to see how far I could get. "Well, I'll be going to my grandmother's in a few, so could I stop by then?"

"You can come to get anything that you want."

Did he say that? Yes, he did, and that was the opening that I needed. "I'll be over there in about an hour. See you then." After I hung up, I freshened up and headed to Jack's house. I saw my grandmother earlier that day and was told to return later for dinner. That's the one thing I loved about the college I went to; my grandmother was only 10 minutes away.

When I arrived at my grandmother's, she was leaving. "Hey, Grandma, where are you going?" I asked as I gave her a hug and a kiss.

"Going to see my boo. Dinner is ready; I put some containers in the refrigerator for you to take back to your dormitory. However, I know you'll still stay, eat, and take the containers. My ride is here; I'll call you when I return." That was code for she was headed to bingo, and I should eat if I wanted, grab the containers, and leave. One thing that wasn't in the code was that I disliked being there without her. I loved talking to her. My grandmother was my actual best friend, and I was my grandmother's baby. She was my maternal grandmother, who migrated to New York from the Bahamas. So I went inside, ate, and called Jack.

"Hey there."

"Where are you?"

"Didn't I tell you I was going to my Grandma's?

"Oh yeah, but tonight is her bingo night. Is she there, or did she leave?"

"She left when I got here. You wanna bring me the CD, or should I come over there?"

"I'll be over there in five minutes."

After I hung up, I headed to my room and noticed that my Grandma had cleaned it. My brother and I have our own rooms at the house. We were her only grandkids, and she spoils us, especially me. I opened up the window just in case we had sex. Wouldn't want her to come into the room, and it smells like ass. I heard the bell and went to open the door. "Damn, you are attractive, Kayla." He said when I opened the door.

Laughing, "You just want some ass."

"No, I'm for real. There's just something about you that is sexy."

"Well, thanks; come on in." I closed and locked the door behind him. "So, where's the CD?

He pulled it from his back pants pocket and handed it to me. "Here you go."

"Great, we can listen to it now," I said as we headed to my bedroom. When we got there, I put it into the CD player, and we made our way over to the bed and sat on it.

"Can I kiss you?"

"What?"

"Can I kiss you?"

"Why?"

"Because I've wanted to do it since the first day I met you."

"If that's what." He kissed me while I was in mid-sentence. He leaned in, kissing me so I could lie on the bed. He took off my shirt and bra, caressed the twins, and teased my nipples with the tip of his tongue; occasionally, he would feast on them. He then kissed his way down to my belly button and took off my pants and thong. He licked

Kay-Kay in a way that made my eyes open wide. He stuck his tongue so far up in her that I couldn't believe it. Well, Kay-Kay and I both couldn't believe it. We didn't know how deep she really was until then. Jack could touch the tip of his nose with his tongue. As he licked, he sucked, and then he did the ultimate. As he licked Kay-Kay, he stuck a finger inside her and up my ass. Believe it or not, that turned me on even more. I was shocked, and Kay-Kay was getting wetter. This bitch literally spazzed out on me. He feathered his fingers inside Kay-Kay and my ass and furiously teased her with his tongue, which sent me over the top.

My body went numb before Kay-Kay squirted on his face. He then infused his penis with Kay-Kay. We fucked to the beat of the music. As Lenny sang, Jack jammed his instrument in Kay-Kay harder. Even though it was wild and crazy, it was good. He flipped me over so that I was riding him. As I rode his cock, he put a finger in my ass and stimulated my anus. My arousal level was off the charts, and Kay-Kay was all for it. I could hear the sound of macaroni and cheese being stirred sound. A bitch was wet!!! The next thing I knew, he pulled out of Kay-Kay, put me on my stomach, arched my hips, and entered my ass with ease. This was my first time having anal sex. It felt like he was still in Kay-Kay, the way he was going in and out. As he fucked me in the ass from behind, he played with Kay-Kay. I just felt her getting wetter. I couldn't believe how good this felt. When I came, I erupted like a volcano; it was the first time that Kay-Kay and I experienced something freaky. I was in la-la land.

"So, what are you thinking about?" He asked as he caressed my breasts.

"Whoa!" I was speechless.

"Is that all you can say?"

"That was unbelievable," I said, out of breath.

"Would you do it again?"

"Tonight?" I asked as I could barely sit up.

"Just, in general?" He asked as his mouth found its way back to Kay-Kay.

"Well, uh." I just gave up my thoughts as he kissed and licked Kay-Kay. He had his tongue skillfully moving around and tormenting her, but in the right way. He would solidify his tongue at the perfect time and then start licking. He made her explode one more time before he went back in. This time, there was no music playing. His movements were slow, long, and steady, and he kept it that way until I exploded again.

"I'm still waiting for your answer."

"Yes, I can do it again."

"Well, how about I come and get the CD, and we do it again?"

"And when will you be coming for the CD?"

"Maybe tomorrow night when you come to visit your grandmother. You can come to my place when you're done, and I can take you back to school."

"Sounds fine, but who says I'm coming here tomorrow? It's my busiest day, and I'm the R.A. on duty tomorrow."

"You're an R.A.?"

"Yep."

"Well, can't you sign me in, and I can leave whenever?" He asked with a smile.

"That I can do." I got up and looked for my clothes. "It's good that I opened up those windows, but I hate it for the person who has to sit next to me on the bus. I smell like pure sex." I said, looking at Jack, who was smiling at me. "Why do you still have that smile on your face?"

"Because I feel good." He then got up and dressed; when he was done, he followed me into the kitchen. Next, I fixed a plate of food for both of us. After we were done, I returned to my room, sprayed Lysol, and closed the windows. Then, I returned to the kitchen, grabbed my already packed food, packed it in the bag, and headed out.

Jack walked me to the bus stop. The bus pulled up, the doors opened, and he kissed me on the cheek and waited to see me sit down. When the bus took off, so did he.

FYI, Jack and I became and remained friends with benefits for a little while after that, but we are still great friends.

CANDY LICKING STALKER

Kayla was sitting with some friends, minding her business at the campus bar, when she finally noticed Mr. Candy Licker Stalker. His real name was Leo, and he had just transferred from another college. Instead of this being his senior year, he was a second-year junior. Kayla passed him several times in the dorm but never paid any attention. Then, he approached the table as she sat with some friends, drinking tap beer. He knew some people at the table but felt the need to talk to Kayla for some reason.

"How are you, Kayla?"

"I'm fine, and you?" She asked nervously.

"I'm good. We have a class together." "We do?"

"Yes, Sociology. I sit in the back by the door, and you sit in the front. My roommate Shawn sits next to you. He says he cheats off of you."

"Yeah, he does. Well, at least he will pass once again, thanks to me. So where's Sean?" She asked.

"He went home for the night but will return for class tomorrow."

Shaking her head, "Lucky him. Well, it was nice to meet you, Leo. I'll see you around." She said bye to everyone else and headed back to the dorms. She couldn't have been more than ten steps away from the front door to the dorm when she heard someone shouting her name. When she looked back to see who it was, it was Leo. "Hey there."

"So, what are you about to do?"

"Why?" She asked curiously.

"I was just asking." He said.

"Well, if you must know. I'm about to shower and then to bed; I wish someone were waiting for me to eat my Ka-Kay." That was me; I didn't want Kayla to have control of this situation.

"Your Kay-Kay?"

"Yes, my pussy."

"Oh, then I'm your guy. Could I taste some of your Kay-Kay?"

Oh no, he didn't ask. "You want to taste some of my Kay-Kay?" She asked, laughing.

"Sure."

"Well, how about I come to your room in about an hour?"

"I'll see you then." So he went his way, and she went to shower.

When Kayla finally reached his room, he opened the door and guided her to his bed. Kayla lay down, and he devoured me. He was very good at what he did. His tongue was extra long like Jack's. So when he went deep, he went deep. He would lick me and then suck on me. His licks were long and deep, or he'd stiffen his tongue and fuck me with it. The next thing I knew, he wrote my and Kayla's names in cursive. Writing our names with his tongue made me extra wet. Kayla had her hands on his head and pushed him further into me. She could only see his eyes. He spread her legs. Placed them behind her head and held them down. His tongue went from the inside of me to her ass back inside me. Her moans got louder as he licked, sucked, and wrote our names a few more times; he and I had an hour-long conversation before I creamed all over his face. When Kayla got up, she could barely walk. "Thanks, Leo."

"No problem. Besides, you taste terrific, so if you ever need that taken care of, you know where I am."

"Thanks." We both knew that she wouldn't be calling him again. One time was good enough. Who decides to sit next to her the next day in class and not by the door? Yeah, Leo. It was like he started to pop up out of the blue. Kayla pays attention to who's around her and never notices Leo. She could now spot him two blocks away. He even came to her room unannounced a few times; naturally, Kayla had to curse him out. She would always have to peek out her door before she left her room. She'd take the stairs some days, but he still managed to stalk her.

He even picked up after Spring Break. He spotted her in the lobby, waiting until she got to her room. She gave it a week, and after that week, security was notified. After that, the stalking was kept to a minimum in class and every now and then in the dorm. Anytime Shawn would invite her to his room, she declined, and when she tutored him, he had to come to her room. Luckily, she graduated, and the stalking stopped. Damn, all he did was have a taste of me; I wonder what would have happened if he had dipped his rod into me?

After I graduated high school, I pretty much just rocked out with Jamal, aka Mr. Toxic. I dibbled and dabbled with Chad during my first year of college. Derrick and I would mess around occasionally, but nothing too serious. We were just fuck buddies when needed. I thought I'd meet my future husband in college, but I didn't. It wasn't until I bumped into Marion that I got into my next "serious" relationship. But, of course, you know how that ended. Here's something entirely out of the blue. Right before I graduated, Marion actually called me at school. I don't know how he got my number, but this call was unexpected and out of the blue. Marion called to tell me he was getting locked up or just sentenced. Something to that extent. And I was like, good, because he wouldn't be able to hurt people the way he did, and I hoped that somebody made him their bitch. He told me I didn't mean it, and I told him I did. After hanging up, I couldn't help but think that's where he needed to be. It's funny because after he went to jail, Marion confessed that he used the product he used to sell before we got into that fight in my room at the dorm. Remember, he was a street pharmacist. After a few letters, I eventually saw him a few times. My first question to him was, "Did anyone make you their bitch yet?" He could see that I was serious.

We kept in touch and grew closer while he was locked up. When he was released, he went to another place, which I think was a halfway house. I also visited him there. Then, when he was finally released, we continued to work on our friendship. Finally, we reached a point where we were comfortable sharing information about our relationships. Well, him more than me. Marion liked younger women whom he could control. He had a problem with women he couldn't control. His family was having a gathering, and instead of inviting his current girlfriend, he asked me. I went. He and his current girlfriend were fighting over a few things. One issue was that she checked his voicemail, so he changed his PIN number in front of me. You know where I'm going with this, right? Yes, occasionally, I'd listen to his voicemail, where I learned he was still a street pharmacist but part-time. I regularly checked and deleted the junkie's voicemails, saying they needed their fix. Yes, I also deleted his girlfriend's messages when I felt petty. Eventually, his ass went back to jail. During that bid, I did not keep in contact with him.

Anywho, now that I'm a college graduate and living in Midtown. I was also stepping into my inner Samantha, my favorite Sex and the City character. I wondered whether my body count would remain the same or go up, and, if so, by how much? Will I meet my future husband? I didn't know what the sexual future looked like for Kay-Kay and me, but we were optimistic about whatever would happen.

COULDA LOST HER LIFE

Every now and then, I like to take a stroll, and when I stroll, there's no telling who I might run into or who I may meet. So, one day, I decided to hop on the train and walk in the city. My first stop was the basketball court on W. 4th St. in the West Village. Standing near the fence, I spotted a burgundy Lincoln Navigator and a handsome driver. So, of course, I made eye contact with him. I also met a guy who owned an African American store on W. 8th St. He asked me to walk with him to the store.

As we walked up W. 8th, we heard a gunshot, and everyone who heard the shot quickly got down on the ground while others ducked between parked cars. As I weaved between two parked cars, I saw the burgundy Navigator passing me. Kay-Kay began to jump. The driver was handsome; did I mention that? Once the chaos had settled, everyone on the street did their business. Come to find out, someone was trying to rob an African vendor, and he wasn't with it. After talking to the store owner, I browsed around the store, and while he wasn't looking, I walked out.

As I was crossing the street, the Navigator was coming back up the street, and as it was coming my way, it slowed down and stopped in front of me. "Excuse me, Miss, but do you know what happened?" The driver asked.

"Someone was stealing from one of the street vendors, and he took matters into his own hands," I said.

"Oh, weren't you just over by the basketball court?" He asked.

"You know I was," I answered sarcastically. "Are you following me?"

"Maybe." He extended his hand, "Hi, my name is David."

Extending my hand to shake his, "Kayla."

"Hi, Kayla, I'm James." Another voice said. James was chillin in the seat that was pushed back and reclined as far as it could go. "My boy here thinks that you got it going on."

"Hi, James, and is that right?" I asked, looking at David.

"Yes, I do. So where are you headed?"

"Nowhere in particular, just on a stroll. Why do you ask?"

"I'm just asking."

"Sure you are," I said with a smile.

"Well, since you aren't doing anything, how about we do something?"

"I don't know you that well."

"Well, here's our chance to get to know each other. So how about it?' I decided to get in the truck and ride with David and James. "I just have to drop him off, and we can go."

"Not a problem."

"Do you have any friends that look like you?" James asked.

"No."

"Why not?"

"Why should I?"

"Pretty girls normally travel in packs."

"Well, not this pretty girl," I said, "I like to travel alone to do what I want. If I had been with someone, I wouldn't be talking or riding with you guys."

"I hear that. I also like that. It means that you aren't scared." David said.

"It doesn't necessarily mean that I'm not scared. It just means that I like to experience life."

"I like that as well," James said as he noticed we were approaching his building. "Well, I'm home now and hope to talk to you again. You're an interesting female."

"Thanks, James." I moved from the backseat to the front." So, where are we headed?"

"I don't know," David said.

"Okay, well, do you have any suggestions?"

"I live in Queens."

"So Queens it is," I said, and what the hell was I thinking when I said that? As we drove, the conversation flowed, and then the unexpected happened. I don't know how, but it did. We were stuck in traffic, so he grabbed some baby oil from the side of the door and put it in the cup holder. He then pulled out his dick. He told me to open my hands as he grabbed the baby oil and opened it. He poured a little in my hands and asked me to oil down his member. I did. We sat in traffic, and I jerked him off. Once traffic started to flow, so did he.

"We drove to his house to pick up some clothes and went to a hotel by LaGuardia airport. He checked us in, and we made our way to the room; we both got comfortable. "I hope you don't mind, but I'm attending a party tonight. But I promise I will come back."

"No problem," I said, but I had money to get home if he didn't, but I was staying in that room with or without him. I wasn't trying to go back home from Queens this late.

He headed into the shower. "Kayla, come here." He shouted. When I got to the door, I saw a stunning body. "Come on in." I took off my clothes and joined him in the shower. He grabbed my hands and pulled me into the shower. This wasn't the first time Kay-Kay and I had sex in the shower, but this time was worth talking about. First, he had me put my hands against the wall, slightly lean over, and then enter from behind. He felt so good inside Kay. David then held my hips while occasionally caressing my ass as he pumped in and out of me. Finally, he turned me over and pinned me against the wall as he held my leg that was wrapped around him. He would put his hand around my neck when he would go deep. The water bounced off our bodies. Kay-Kay must have felt really good to him because his body started jerking.

He picked me up, carried me to the bed, and put on another condom. He had my legs every which way as he was on top of me. It felt good, and I think my legs got a good workout. First, he had them on his shoulders while working with Kay-Kay. Next, he wrapped one leg around his waist with the other on his shoulder. Next thing I knew, my legs were behind my head; his hands pressed down my thighs as he dipped in and out of Kay-Kay. Finally, he flipped me over and entered from behind. I kept throwing Kay-Kay on his rod, and he couldn't handle it. His body began to jerk hard and fast; he fell on top of me and then rolled onto the bed. "Damn, that was good." After lying there for twenty minutes, he eventually got up and dressed. "Please be here when I get back." He said before he walked out the door.

"I can't make you any promises, but I'll try." He left; I lay on the bed and decided to shower, order room service, and watch a few movies. I fell asleep during the second movie. When I woke up in the middle of the night, I noticed David had returned. I quietly got up that morning and left him to sleep in the room. When I got downstairs, I had the front desk clerk call me a cab. I took a cab to the nearest train station and went home.

Once on the train, I began to think about what had just happened. I got in a car with a stranger and went to Queens, not knowing what could happen. Had sex with a said stranger, and when he came back to the room, he could have done something to me, and nobody would have known. I could have really lost my life for the third time.

The first time I almost lost my life, I was home from college and drinking at a local bar. A guy was watching me, and after a while, he came over and started a conversation. We talked a little before he bought me a drink. He then asked if he could take me home, and my drunk ass said yes. He kept asking me if I was ready to go for the next hour, and I wasn't. I eventually got tired of him asking, so I said yes. Before leaving, I told Breezy I was going and showed him who was there so he would recognize the guy. When we walked to his car, another guy was there. We got to the car, and I went to open the back door, but the other guy told me to sit in the front. I did. He took a left instead of a right out of the parking lot, as I had directed him to my house. At that moment(say that like Morgan Freeman), I told myself to get out of the car at the next light. I could see that the door wasn't locked, and he was driving slowly. As he approached a light that just turned red, thank goodness, I opened the door, jumped out,

The second time, I was in college and went to a club with some friends, and I met a guy, and we exchanged numbers. For some reason, he was fascinated with my nose. I was at a friend's house in Brooklyn when he paged me. I returned his call, and he picked me up an hour later. We drove to Queens….smh. I smoked, so he got me some weed and a pack of Backwoods, and we headed to a hotel. After checking in, we went to the room. I rolled up, lit my blunt, and we talked as I smoked.

I was on the bed, and he was in a chair, and then he sat next to me on the bed. He went to kiss me, and I pulled back. He said we couldn't fuck, and I said, Okay, no problem. His reason was that he didn't want to cheat on his fiancée or some shit. But he was like, I could suck his dick, no sir! He got a little aggressive when I told him I wasn't sucking his dick, so I said, Okay, let me go use the bathroom. Thank goodness the door was by the bathroom. I was trying to figure out how the fuck I was going to leave without sucking dick; I wasn't there yet and didn't feel safe. I figured it out. I flushed the toilet, came out, and noticed he couldn't see me from where he was. I turned the water on and started talking loudly. As the water was running and I spoke very loudly, I made some noise as I unlocked the door, opened it, and ran to the closest exit as fast as possible. I still had my lil backpack on, so I wasn't leaving anything behind.

I had to run back to where I had come from to get out of the parking lot and onto the main road. I felt like Tina Turner after she escaped from Ike in the movie, but I hadn't been beaten, and there was no dry blood on my face. I was in Queens, so I was fucked. I got far enough to a bus stop, got on it, and was headed to a train station I'd later become familiar with. My pager kept going off the whole time, but it didn't stop. I didn't know the number, and I wasn't going to find out who was calling me. But what could have happened if I stayed and didn't suck homeboy off…

I be wilding….

MR. WHAM

Shay lived a few houses down from Kayla's mother, and they were cool with each other. He never disrespected her; he'd take her out whenever she wanted to go, whether she was home from school or just visiting her mother. So many people thought they were a couple because they were always together, even though they were good friends. Kayla was at her mother's house for the weekend. On Friday night, she got there and went over to his house. I was curious to see what he was all about, so I put together a plan. Of course, Kayla had just finished smoking, so she was high. I was going to get Kayla to get him open. She knew he drank, so she would go to his place, chill, and drink with him. She called to make sure that he was home, and he was. "Hello."

"What's up, Shay?"

"Nothing; why do you want to go out?"

"No. Can I come over?"

"You know you don't have to ask."

"Yes, I do. You might have company, and you know that's not how I get down."

"Even if I had company, I'd tell them to leave."

"If you say so. I'm headed over there now." *She hung up and walked a few houses down. When she got there, she got straight to the point.* "Shay, do you have anything to drink?"

"Anything like what?"

"Do you have any beer, wine, vodka, or tequila?"

"Well, since you just graduated, why not have some Moet?"

"You don't have to open the Moet. Instead, you can save that for something or someone special."

"It's okay, and besides, you're special and officially a college graduate."

"Okay, well, if you insist," Kayla laughed. "Shay, can I ask you a question?"

"Sure." He said as he opened up the bottle of Moet."

"How come you never tried to get in my pants?"

"What?" He asked, surprised.

"Oh, you heard me. I don't think I need to repeat myself."

"Trust me when I say that; I want to, but since I've gotten to know you, I like you, and I wouldn't want to risk ruining our friendship."

"Very interesting and understandable. I had sex with a friend once, and now we barely speak. He was actually one of my best friends."

"Why, you ask?" He asked as he handed her a glass of Moet.

"Just thought I would, that's all." She held up her glass. "Let's toast." He brought his glass up to hers. "Congratulations to me on graduating and our friendship."

"Congrats and to friendship." *They both took sips.* "You wanna watch a movie?"

"Sure." *He popped in a movie that neither one was paying attention to.* "Do you have a girlfriend?"

"Why do you ask?"

"Hell, whenever I came home from school and when you got off work, it's like we always end up together. And I've never seen you with any other female besides me, your mom, or your sister."

"Well, I don't." He gulped down the rest of his Moet and poured himself another glass. "You dance?"

"You've seen me at the club. I get down." She said as she stood up and began to dance.

Laughing. "Actually, I never see you until it's time to go. So I wouldn't really know if you can dance or not."

My plan was going well; he was tipsy. "You want to dance?" She asked.

"Sure, what should I put on?"

"Reggae." *That way, she could grind on him and see what he's working with. He walked over to the stereo and found some reggae music to put on. She walked over to him and began to gyrate her hips against him. Then, she turned around and grinded on him until she felt him getting hard. He kissed her neck, grabbed her waist, walked her over to the couch, and threw her down. He took off her sweatpants and practically ripped off her shirt. As he kissed her breasts, he not only bit her hard, but he also sucked hard. He pulled out his manhood, which was very hard. He was between her legs when he pulled it out. I was kind of afraid of it. He tapped me with it. Who does that? He was hard and ready to go. When he placed himself inside me, it felt like he just pushed his way in. His movements were not too fast but very hard. He would slam his manhood into me over and over again. There was no rhythm. After ten minutes of slamming, he helped her up, slammed her against the wall, wrapped one leg around his waist, and returned inside me. Once again, he was attacking me with his spear. He then threw her onto the bed and began stabbing the fuck out of me. He had her legs over his shoulders and slam, slam, slam. Finally, he turned her so that he could enter from the back. After about six good, hard blows, he was done.*

As he lay there sleeping, Kayla struggled to find her clothes. She remembered her experience with Caleb and how she couldn't walk afterward, but this wasn't as good as that experience. I think Shawn was better, and I hope Kayla chooses Shawn if given a choice between Shay and Shawn. Thank goodness Kayla lived four houses away, because my girl couldn't walk; she practically crawled home. But, of course, that night was my fault because she went straight to bed and didn't check on me until late afternoon the next day.

What the fuck do I be thinking? I know I'm stepping into my inner Samantha, but I need a better dick radar. Shay doesn't make her jump, but he makes us curious. I need a radar on my glasses that scans for dick size, oral capabilities, and performance. This guy here was a complete dud. My pussy should not be feeling like this.

Here's where I become unsmart:

I only saw the shit I was about to experience in Lifetime movies. I didn't think they could possibly happen in real life. Little did I know. If someone had told me I was about to star in and live in my Lifetime movie, I would never have believed them... So here's my story: Let's call it *The Tale of Two Men*... We were at the train station, he was coming into the city, and I was leaving. When we were close enough, we made eye contact instantly. His name was Tyler; he was about six feet five inches tall, had an athletic build, dusty brown, reddish hair, and light skin, and he had freckles under his eyes, nose, and cheeks. He played basketball overseas. Smiling at each other was the start of our conversation. Naturally, he asked me my height and if I played basketball. Basketball, no; volleyball, yes. He asked me where I was going, and I told him I was going home for the weekend. He guessed that I went to college in the city; he then asked me what school I went to, and I told him. I found out we had mutual friends. Chad and his roommate were his friends. After our brief conversation, we went our separate ways. I thought that was my last time seeing him. Fast forward to just a month after graduation, and I run into Tyler again. I was meeting up with someone who just happened to be standing next to Tyler and a guy he was talking to.

Furthermore, we made eye contact and were shocked to see each other. Again, he approached me after he finished his conversation. This time, we exchanged numbers and hung out. Tyler was a gentleman. We had fun together, and I appreciated our conversations. Whenever we met up, we would go on long walks. Because of the conversation, it didn't seem like we had walked thirty city blocks. He showed me that he cared, and I could tell he cared.

There's Vaughn; we knew each other, but not really. However, we eventually exchanged numbers, and well...

MR. FANTASY

I was at The Cage in the West Village when I first looked at Vaughn, who was 6'7 "tall, with an athletic build and a mocha skin tone. He was a basketball player. His sexy gray eyes were mesmerizing. We later learned that those were contacts. This was the first time I saw a man, and I became speechless. I could talk when I saw Caleb, but there were no words for Vaughn. I couldn't even say hello. Any other time, I could start a conversation with a guy I found attractive and was sexually curious about with no problems. But, for some reason, this was different. He made me nervous.

"So, which one of these guys is your man?" I heard a voice coming from behind me ask.

"None," I replied without turning around.

"So, can I get your number?"

That made me turn around, and when I did, I was shocked. "Excuse me?"

"I asked you for your number, but I have a better idea. How about we exchange numbers?" That's what we did. "I have a game here tomorrow at three. I hope that I get to see you."

"I'll be here." I watched him as he walked away. I couldn't help but shake my head. He was a sexy man. After he was out of sight, I looked at my phone and realized we hadn't exchanged names, so I saved him as SEXY. "Kay-Kay, you alright?" *Her panties were sticking to me as I began to throb. The throbbing was me telling her, "Yes, girl, it's okay. He is sexy, so if you want to fuck him, I'm all in."*

The next day, I watched him play on the basketball court. After the game, he grabbed his things and came over to stand next to me. After dropping his bag on the ground, he looked at me. "Thanks for coming." Before I could say anything, he kissed me. I wasn't one to kiss someone I wasn't involved with, but I kindly accepted his tongue. He then pulled back, "Come home with me."

Shocked, "Uh, where do you live?"

"Queens."

"What the fuck?" I said to myself as I thought about my Queens experiences, but decided to go anyway. He picked his bag up, and we headed toward the train station. Once we were on the train, we found seats and sat down. He then sang Can You Stand The Rain by New Edition, which I love and hate at the same damn time. He stroked my face during the train ride and kissed me occasionally. Once we finally made it to Queens, we got off the train, and it looked familiar. It was the station I ended up at after my previous experience in Queens. We had to take a bus, which let us off in front of his place. After I signed in, we headed to his apartment.

When we got inside, he dropped his bag, turned around, and planted another kiss on my lips. He carried me to the couch, removed my sneakers and socks, and pulled off my shorts. He sucked and licked my toes, and then he greeted Kay-Kay with his tongue; this was our first experience with a tongue ring. He made us feel so good. Vaughn gave her the sweetest, softest French kiss. He played with her with his tongue ring, and as she got wet, he stopped and left me lying on the couch. "Don't move." I didn't; hell, I couldn't. He went into the shower.

I sat up on my elbows, "Bitch did he just lick you like that and then just leave us here?" *I started throbbing.* "I take that as a yes." I lay back down with my forearm on my forehead, placed my free hand on Kay-Kay, patted her, and eventually dozed off. The day before, I went to the Bronx with a friend; yes, we were fuck buddies. We watched the Chris Rock comedy special and then fucked. I got up early, went to my place, showered, changed, and headed to his game. I didn't get any sleep, so I was tired.

When he finished his shower, he must have come out of the bathroom and lit the candles. He got me off the couch and led us to the bedroom, where there were more lit candles. He lay me down and kissed every inch of my body, starting at my toes and working his way up. *When he got to me, I was still flustered from when he greeted me before going into the shower. He began to kiss and lick her inner thighs, drawing himself closer to me without touching me. As he got closer with his licks and kisses, he ran his fingers inside the crease of my outer lips and her thighs. The next thing I knew, he began kissing and licking me. He licked, kissed, and sucked. Sucked, kissed, and licked. Kissed, sucked, and licked. My walls were drenched. He slowly moved up to her breasts while placing his member inside me....OH BOY!!!!*

When he entered me, Kayla and I were both happy. It felt like, in me, was where he belonged. As he stroked her, he looked into my eyes, and I never looked away. *I know she didn't look away because of how my wetness was set up. It felt so damn good the way he stroked me.* Instead of somebody going at me for the first time, he made love to me.

Derrick was my boyfriend who never made love to me. Shit, I don't think he knew how, but he fucked me just right. Back to Vaughn, his strokes were long and slow. *He would bury himself in me and occasionally move around in circular motions with gentle thrusts. Even though he was inside me, it felt like he was humping me at times. Then, just as I thought I would cum, he'd change his motions and return to the long, slow strokes.* We started at six that evening, and when I looked at the clock, it was a bit after nine when we finished.

It was eleven o'clock when I woke up. I was, like, oh shit! But when I looked out the window, I could see it was dark. It felt like I had been sleeping all night. I couldn't believe that I had been asleep for only two hours. Told you I was tired. Before I could turn over, I felt Vaughn kissing the back of my neck, making his way to the front. *Oh yes, once again, it was on and popping. He came right back down to kiss me. I truly felt how Kayla felt when he kissed her. He made me wetter than ever; I just tingled; my 'sweat' never hit the bed. I sweated in his mouth, and I could hear him slurp it all up. Once again, he entered and began the slow, long strokes. When he finished, he just lay there throbbing inside of me.* Yeah, we didn't use a condom.

When I woke up the following day, I woke up to his tongue inside me. He was so deep inside of me that it woke Kayla up. She must have thought she was dreaming until she opened her eyes and saw that he was between her legs. His tongue fucked me so well that I had a little trouble keeping up with him initially, but eventually, I found and got into his groove. Once he realized I was wetter than wet, he stopped, flipped Kayla over, arched her hips, and re-entered me. He held onto Kayla's hips as he went in and out. When he let go, Kayla kept up with him. As he gave it to her, she threw me back on his dick. The harder she threw me back on his dick, the louder his moans were. Kayla then got on her knees as he was still inside of me. While on one knee, she straightened her other leg to the side. He grabbed her hips and began to slam me on his dick. After the slamming, he began to pump me hard, and Kayla slammed me on his dick. She slammed, he pumped, and we all came together. That had to have been one of the best nuts for us. Thank goodness I didn't have to work until eleven that morning. I had time to go home, shower, and work on time.

When I arrived, Tyler called and asked if we could meet for lunch. Since they were remodeling the offices, I didn't have to be there all day, so I agreed. We only worked three blocks apart, so it wasn't a problem. We met in what we considered the middle, which happened to be in front of a Subway store. We went inside and ordered. As we were ordering, the server complimented us. He thought we looked good together. He then began a conversation with Tyler. "Is that your girlfriend?" Tyler looked at me before answering, and I smiled, then looked at the server to make sure he wasn't someone I fucked and fucked over. He wasn't; I never saw him before.

Still smiling and looking at me, "Yes, she is."

"You two look perfect together." The server replied.

"Thank you, I plan on marrying her one day," Tyler said.

Looking at him, shocked, "What did you just say?"

"You heard me," he said. We headed to a table to sit and eat. "I have a five-year plan for us."

"Is that right?"

"Yes, these first two years we date, get to know each other. In year three, we get engaged; by year four, we move in together; in year five, we get married." He said with no hesitation.

"Well, I see you have this all figured out, but your plan has one problem."

Intensely looking into my eyes, "What's the problem?"

"Me, being on board with your plan."

"You will be, I have no doubts about that." He said as he took another bite of his sandwich. I just shook my head as I took a sip of my drink.

After lunch, Tyler walked me back to my job and headed back to his. When he got back there, he called me, and we talked on the phone for the rest of the day. After work, I went home, showered, and went to bed.

The next day, Vaughn called me. "Hey there, what are you doing?"

"Hey, I'm just getting off work. Why, what's up?" I asked with a smile, hoping he would say he wanted to see me.

"Could you meet me somewhere?"

Jackpot. "Where?"

"How about we meet at BBQ's on W. 8th St. in about an hour?"

"Meet you then." I closed my cell phone and called Tyler. Tyler was someone I could have settled down with. He had a plan, and I respected that; I liked Vaughn's dick better and was hooked. Tyler's dick wasn't that bad; it was long and fat, but had a fur coat that turned me off. I could have sex with him if he kept his shirt on, but I like the skin-to-skin feeling. Other than that, he was perfect; again, he was a man with a plan. Because Vaughn's dick was better, I switched Tyler from option one to option two. "Hey, Tyler, what's up?"

"Nothing on my way to see you."

"Damn, that's right, we had plans today to meet up. I completely forgot. I have to stay and work overtime and don't know how long I will be." First lie.

"If it's not that late, maybe we can meet later?"

"Are you sure?" I asked.

"Yes. Call me when you're done, and I'll meet you at the train station. So you make that money, and I'll see you later."

"Tyler, are you sure?"

"Yes, love, I am. Again, make that money, and I'll see you later." He hung up. I closed my phone, smiling. I was hoping to get my groove on. I looked at my watch and realized I had to hurry to catch the train if I didn't want to be late. When I got to the train station, a train was pulling up. I got on and made my way to the Village. I got off the train and ran/walked up W. 8th St., where I saw Vaughn standing outside the restaurant.

We made our way inside and enjoyed our meal. When we left, we headed to the Pink Pussycat on W. 4th, then back up to Christopher St. and into the Treasure Chest. After browsing around in both stores, we headed to Central Park. We made our way to Umpire Rock, where you could see kids running and chasing each other on the rocks and grass. I was wearing my little denim shirt dress, which was perfect for the occasion. Vaughn dropped his bag on the rocks and then lay down, resting his head on the bag and his legs bent. I dropped my bag beside him, straddled across him, and rested my back on his thighs. As I was on top of him, he placed himself inside Kay-Kay. What made this moment intense was that nobody knew what was really happening. My little dress hid what we were doing well. As he was inside Kay-Kay, she would tighten up her muscles. Every now and then, I would move up and down, but nobody knew what was happening. Finally, we had to leave because we all wanted to go all out and get into the flow. We got up and headed back to his place.

When we got there, he headed into the shower. When he came out, he played some music, and we danced. After the dance, it was on and poppin'. He led me to the bedroom and lay me down. He had a bag sitting on the nightstand that he had gone into. He grabbed a blindfold out of it and placed it over my eyes. Next, he pulled all the contents back out of the bag. He poured oil on my body, massaged it into my skin and other parts; he licked it off. I then felt a small whip touch my body. He ran it all over my body, and as he did that, Kay-Kay got wetter than she already was. He then began to tickle her with the feather, and after that, he went for the gusto. *He inserted something inside me that didn't feel like a real dick. It was too hard, and I could tell I wasn't accustomed to it.*

As it went in and out, it turned, and no dick goes in and out and turns. Also, there's no way he could lick and kiss me with his dick inside.

It drove Kayla crazy. Her legs started shaking, and the floodgates opened. After the waterfall, Vaughn got up, went into the kitchen, and returned with some Vanilla Fudge Swirl ice cream, which was very good. He let me feed him some, then feed myself. I put some ice cream on his manhood and began to lick it off. I then had him all in my mouth and sucked on the tip as I stroked him up and down. Finally, I flicked my tongue around the head and surrounded my mouth around his penis. I sucked him until he was hard, and once he knew he was hard, he pulled me up and had me slide Kay-Kay down his staff. Then, with my knees by his side, I rode him like there was no tomorrow. He held me by my hips and would slam me down on his dick; when I said it, it felt good. It felt so damn good. It didn't take either of us that long to cum, and when we did, we just kept going until we came for the second time, and we both fell asleep. Needless to say, I forgot all about Tyler.

It's good that my summer bags were totes, making it easy to travel with 'just in case' clothes, because Vaughn's alarm woke me up. We got ready for work and headed out the door. When we got to the train, we kissed and touched each other a lot, waking Kay-Kay up. She either jumped or made my panties wetter than they were every time he felt me. Before I got off the train, I was ready to have sex with him right then and there. He kissed me and whispered, "Meet me at the pizza shop by the basketball court when you get off work. I got off the train and headed to my job.

During my lunch break, I met up with Tyler, whom I had forgotten about the night before. Although I came to think about it, I didn't think about him. He never said anything about it. We were always thrilled to see each other. We had fun no matter what we did. For lunch, we went back to Subway.

After lunch, I returned to the office, where Vaughn's message reminded me to meet him at the pizza shop. So, when I got off work, I headed straight to the pizza shop.

Vaughn finished his slice when I arrived and told me to follow him. I followed him right into the bathroom. We entered the first stall; he closed the door behind him, turned me around, pulled up my dress, and pulled my thong to the side. He turned my head and kissed me. Then, he pulled his pants down, pulled his dick out, and entered Kay-Kay from the back. As Vaughn hit it from the back, he'd go in and out or hump me from behind as he played with Kay-Kay. I bit my lip so hard that I started to bleed. I could taste the blood. It was either that or letting out loud moans. I could tell he was about to come because he was hitting it extra hard and having a hard time holding back his moans. Again, this was an intense episode because we were in a public bathroom. Once we were done, when we walked out, if people had been waiting, they could have put two and two together. Lucky for us, no one was in the waiting area. After we came, we exited the bathroom and went to the basketball court. As he stood behind me and draped his jacket backward over me, he was able to maneuver his hand between the buttons of my dress and put a finger inside Kay-Kay. Boy, what a feeling!! Vaughn and I became a weekend thing, but always spoke on the phone. At night, when he heard songs that reminded him of me, he'd call and let me listen. That made me smile and her wet. One Saturday night, while I was on a girls' night out, he called to say he wanted to see me the next day. Of course, I agreed. The following day, I got up early, did what I had to do, and was on my way. When I got off the train, I noticed a few messages and checked them. They were all from Vaughn, who couldn't wait to see me.

I got off the bus too early but not too far from Vaughn's place, so I walked. I decided to stop by the store and pick up some strawberries. These strawberries were the most unusual. Not only were they extra fat, but they were long. They were actually the same length as someone's thumb or pinky finger. I was amazed, so I purchased them. When I got to Vaughn's building, the doorman didn't make me sign in since he always saw me there. So I called Vaughn when I got off the elevator on his floor. When I got to his door, it was already open. He greeted me with a hug and a passionate kiss; he took my bags and put them in his bedroom. I went into the kitchen and cleaned the strawberries. He came into the kitchen, and he, too, couldn't believe how long they were. He took them from me and led me to the living room.

He sat on the couch, and Kayla stood before him, undressing. The next thing she knew, she was on her back, lying on the sofa. He spread her legs apart and put a strawberry in his mouth. With that strawberry, he played with and teased me. He then placed the strawberry inside me. The strawberry was bigger than Harold because I felt that strawberry move in and out of me; Kayla moved with him as he fucked me with that piece of fruit. I must admit that it felt good. He worked me with that strawberry until I came. Then, he and Kayla ate that strawberry. I know it was extra juicy and sweet. I got up from lying on the couch and had him stand before me, and I took him into my mouth. I sucked and kissed his rod. I would suck on the tip before taking him all in my mouth and moving my tongue around it. I could feel him growing harder and harder in my mouth. I returned to the tip and sucked on it before engulfing him again. As I sucked, I jerked. "Oh, baby, I'm about to come." I heard him say. I sucked and jerked until I could taste his juices.

"Mmmm," I said as he fell beside me on the couch. He pulled me on top of him. I felt like I could sleep on top of him and be comfortable. Unfortunately, I would move the wrong way on purpose. We always had a ball on his couch. The next thing I knew, he had one of my legs draped over the back of the sofa and one over his shoulder, pumping Kay-Kay. He'd play with her as he went in and out. When we flipped over, I was sitting on top, and instead of holding me down by the hips, he took each of my ass cheeks into his hands and just whammed us down on his dick. This was some intense sex.

Our next weekend over at his place was pretty impressive. As usual, he greeted me at the door with a hug and kiss. Next, he took my bags and put them in his room. This time, he held my hand, and I followed. As we kissed each other, we stripped. He then held my hands against the wall and fucked me from behind. Next, he turned me around and wrapped one of my legs around his waist as I leaned back on the wall, and he fucked the shit out of me. I thought I would fall a few times cause my leg was getting weak, but he had me. The next thing I know, he picks me up; I wrap my arms around his neck, and my legs are wrapped around his waist as he bounces me up and down on his dick. We then made our way over to the window.

It was January, so you know it was cold outside, but I don't think we cared. After putting me down, Vaughn grabbed the comforter off the bed, opened the window, and went out on the fire escape. He reached his hand out to me so that I could join him. The fire escape wasn't that big. It was just big enough for people to move from top to bottom in case of a fire. This fire escape was also located in a strange area. Let's say whoever was parking their cars could see us. If anybody looked out of their windows in the other apartment building, they could see us getting it on. That thought didn't stop us, and we gave them something to watch.

Vaughn sat on the steps, the comforter wrapped around him, and I sat in his lap with my back to him. Naturally, he placed himself inside of me. I held on to the rail as I went up and down; Kay-Kay flexed her muscles. He then got up and hit it from behind. I couldn't take it because I felt I was going over with one good hit from behind as he got into it. He understood my concern, and we went back inside. When we got in, we made our way to the bed. I was bent over as he continued hitting it from behind; I then got into the doggy-style position, and he entered. This is where it gets interesting. Vaughn knew about Tyler, but Tyler didn't know of Vaughn. As Vaughn was behind me, he picked up the phone and handed it to me. "Call him and tell him you don't want him."

I was in shock, but at the same time, I found myself dialing his number, really dialing it. When the answering machine came on, I hung up. "Nobody picked up." Thank goodness!!

"Well, when you speak to him, tell him you don't want him." He said as he was still pumping me from behind. I didn't respond. He moved me from the bed, and we stood in the center of the bedroom. He had me bent over, touching my toes. We were in that position for fifteen minutes, and on the fifteenth minute, it was over.

I saw Vaughn on and off until the middle of the following summer. We spent a little over a year "together." He'd do things that pushed me away, and I'd run to Tyler, but then he had a way of pulling me back in. Yes, the dick was that good! I eventually had to walk away from whatever that was and went to Tyler. I started feeling guilty, and ultimately, I told Tyler about Vaughn. After I told him about Vaughn, Tyler didn't speak to me.

I can't lie; there's not a day that goes by that I don't think about Vaughn, and there hasn't been a night that I haven't dreamt of him. So, even though it was just fantastic sex, there was an explainable connection. But it all had to come to an end.

So Vaughn and I were both waiting for rides, and I remember him saying if he wasn't waiting for a ride, he'd take me across the street to the bathroom and fuck me. Just as he made that statement, my ride pulled up, and I told him he didn't have it like that anymore. I got up from where I was sitting and headed towards my ride.

He called me a few days later and told me about his new business venture. It was one of those pyramid schemes. After he told me about it, I told him I wasn't interested, wished him the best, and asked him not to call me anymore. He didn't.

When he pushed me away, he pushed me away. When he pulled me in, well, he did just that. But I was always there for him. One Sunday, something happened at the basketball court, and a mutual friend told me about the incident. He called me asking if I had heard from Vaughn, and I told him I hadn't. Later that same day, I went to the basketball court, and another person told me about the same incident. I called Vaughn a few times before he finally picked up. I asked him if he wanted me to come over. He did; I left and headed to Queens. He greeted me at the door and walked me to the couch. It seemed like all he wanted was to be held, and that's what I did. We eventually had our fun couch time. It was weird, because he kept hiding his left ankle under the couch cushions. Vaughn finally took it out. He was hiding an ankle bracelet that wasn't the jewelry-store ankle bracelet. It was the one that tracked your whereabouts. I said nothing. That incident must have been severe. And still, I didn't ask or say anything. I felt he would if he wanted to share, but he didn't. I left it alone.

There was a time I was going away, and when I got off work, instead of hanging out with Tyler, I met up with Vaughn for coffee and went on my way. About five minutes later, he called my phone, asking to speak to another chick. My response was, Wow, really?! I guess he realized who he had called and hung up. He didn't say a word; he just hung up. While waiting for my flight the next day, he called me. I was talking to him, asking what he wanted from me. I told him other guys wanted to be with me, but I chose him, and he could be replaced. He was playing stupid like that phone call didn't happen the day before, which was pissing me off even more. I mean, at this point, come up with a lie. Say you thought you were calling your co-worker or a relative, something. Don't just act like it didn't happen. I was so nasty. My best friend Breezy was sitting across from me, reading the newspaper. He put the paper down, looked at me, and asked who was still on the phone with me? Breezy said he would have hung up on me already. Vaughn talked about how he loved me—only me —and told me everything I wanted to hear. When it was time to board the flight, I told him I'd call him when I landed. When I got to my destination, I never called Vaughn, but he called me every day, wanting to know when I would return. When I got back home, I was doing laundry when he called and asked if he could see me. I met up with him after he got off work later that night. After we fucked I was like, how do I make you feel? Why do you push me away? The questions were coming at him, and he answered them as I wanted him to, but did he mean it? Nope.

When we were together, we were good, at least that's what I thought. But at the end of the day, I had to walk away from whatever we had. Had I stayed in whatever it was, I would have been emotionally fucked up. I didn't want to walk away, but I had to. I compared the relationship to falling and scraping my knee, and how I cared for the scar would determine how I healed. Either the scab would leave a scar, or if I took care of it and put some cocoa butter on it, there would be no sign of imperfection. And that's what I did by walking away. I took care of my scar, leaving no reminder of the relationship. But again, I did think about and dream about him occasionally.

After getting over Vaughn, I began to focus on Tyler, but I'd feel funny every time we got together. The funny feeling was how could I look this guy in the eyes and be honest with him? I never lied to him, but I kept that I was fucking with someone else from him; I figured, well, since that didn't work out, he didn't have to know. That funny feeling soon turned into guilt. This guy had a five-year plan for us. He saw himself proposing and marrying me. So I had to come clean. Whenever we were together, I'd try to tell him, but I couldn't.

Eventually, I told him. How? I wrote him a letter and mailed it, but I didn't hear from him after he got it. Finally, Tyler crossed my mind, and I decided to call him. A woman answered, and when I told her my name, and she recognized me. Fuuuuuuuuuuuuuuck! She was his fiancée. I told her I just wanted to see how he was; he is engaged to you, so he's okay. No need to say to him, I called. I closed my phone, poured myself a glass of wine, sat on my couch, and turned on the television.

I wasn't focused on it. My attention was on that bottle of wine and the thought of how I could have been Tyler's fiancé, but nope, I had to be honest and tell him. So after I finished the bottle of wine, I went to bed. After dealing with Marion and going through what I went through with Vaughn and Tyler, I decided to focus on myself. I didn't understand how someone could look you in the eye and tell you everything you want to hear, and it all be a lie. I knew because I was doing it to Shawn; I never told him the truth. I also realized that I didn't heal from Marion. I was fucking somebody else the day after Marion and I broke up. And I was in something more than just fucking with Darron. I had never been by myself. So I was gonna focus on me, but make sure Kay-Kay was taken care of.

Years later, Vaughn and I actually reconnected on Facebook. We talked on the phone, texted, and even Skyped. Whenever he got involved with someone, he would stop calling, and I understood that, but I felt he could have said something since we were starting over and were just friends. So, I would be on Facebook, see it, and put it together. Then, he'd reach out to me when the relationships were over. I remember one conversation we had. I was boarding a flight;

he asked me if I believed in polygamy, and I told him that as long as I could have a boyfriend/husband, there would be a problem if I couldn't. My answer ended that conversation.

I'm on the 'Book a few days later and see he's engaged. I congratulated him on the post and even 'loved' the post. The polygamy conversation now made sense. A year after Vaughn got married, he reached out to me. He was going to D.R. and had a layover in New York. I picked him up from the airport, took him to his hotel, we fucked, and I left. We like each other's pictures on Facebook, and that's about it. He started a travel business, and I wasn't interested. To me, it was like a pyramid scheme. I wasn't interested and had other things on my plate. So now we're just friends who like each other's posts and keep it moving. Occasionally, he might comment; when he does, I like his comments and keep them moving. As for Tyler, I hope he's doing well.

I DON'T THINK SO

I've known Matt since high school. I had a crush on his older brother. Matt always teased me because I wasn't like the other girls in high school. Well, I was tomboyish and wore clothes three times my size, so you couldn't tell if I had tits and ass, which I did. Growing up, one of my breasts was more significant than the other. My dad pointed that out jokingly, but it still made me uncomfortable. Derrick didn't have a problem with it, but I got comfortable with my body as I got older. After graduating from college and working in the city, I'd run into Matt occasionally. We had decent conversations.

The first time I saw him, I was working at my first job after college. I was headed to catch a train when, halfway down the train station stairs, I heard someone call my name. When I turned around, I saw Matt standing at the top of the steps. "Hey, Matt." He headed down the steps, and we hugged. "What's going on?"

"I saw you two days ago, but I wasn't sure it was you. Then yesterday, I saw you walk by my job, and I was like, That's you. But today, I thought I'd make sure it was you."

Shocked. "Wow. I actually work two blocks down." I said, pointing in the direction of my job.

"Well, maybe one day we can have lunch."

"Sure. I don't mean to be rude, but I must meet someone. Give me a call, though." I went into my bag to get something to write with and on. I wrote down my number and gave it to him.

Taking the paper with the number on it. "Cool, okay, so I'll give you a call, a call, and maybe we can do lunch?"

"That sounds like a plan." I gave him a hug. "Talk to you soon."

That was the last time that I saw Matt. I had changed jobs and was no longer two blocks away. As I was standing in my new job's reception area talking to the receptionist, the elevator doors opened, and there stood Matt. "Hey there, Matt," I said, surprised.

"I saw you get into the elevator yesterday, and I asked the security guard if you worked in the building, and he told me which floor. I actually work two floors up."

"Let me find out you are following me," I said, laughing. "Well, maybe now we can actually do lunch." I handed him one of the business cards. "Here's my card. Give me a call when you are ready."

"Great. How about tomorrow?" He asked, turning to the elevator

"I take lunch at one."

"Perfect, I'll see you then." He entered the elevator when the doors opened, and I returned to work.

The next day, we met in the lobby for lunch, and over lunch, we were able to catch up. So, naturally, we flirted a little with each other.

After the lunch date, we spoke on the phone; he always told me how he could do this and that sexually, but it went in one ear and out the other.

A few weeks later, we met up for drinks after work. Two martinis in, I invited Matt back to my place. We grabbed a cab and took it to my home. When we arrived, I jumped into the shower, smoked a joint, hit my trusty bong, and freshened up. I made us drinks, and we talked for a bit. Then I was ready. The weed was kicking in. "Look, we know why you're here, so let's get to it," I said as I led him to my bedroom.

He was shocked —or at least he pretended to be. He watched me take off my clothes, get into bed, and did the same. Then, he went straight to Kay-Kay. I felt nothing as he was doing whatever he was doing down there. Kay-Kay didn't get wet or even throb. I tried to get into it, but I couldn't. "Stop. Do you have a condom?" I asked, tapping him on the head.

"Yes."

"Put that on and do what you do." I watched him as he put the condom on and slid in. As he moved, I tried to move with him. I still didn't feel anything. By the time we got to my place, I had sobered up, so I smoked and hit my bong. Typically, I get horny after I smoke. It failed me or was failing me. I kept trying to move with him, but nothing was working. "Stop."

"What's wrong?"

"This is not working. Normally, when I have sex with someone, I'm sexually attracted to that person. So I figured I would smoke and do it without being sexually attracted to you, but it's not happening."

"I thought you were into it when I was down there." He said, pointing with his head.

No, he didn't point it out with his head. "As I said, I was trying to get into it, but no."

"Damn, I've never had anyone tell me I don't do anything for them."

"Well, there's a first for everything," I said, touching his shoulder. "Well, even though it didn't work out this way, we're still cool," I said with a smile.

"Damn, I don't know what to say after that. I guess, I'm sorry."

"Don't be sorry. Just look at it as if we weren't meant to have sex. We're only meant to be friends. Nothing more, nothing less.

FRIEND & LOVER

I've known Lance since junior high school. When we first met, we hit it off and became great friends. As we got older, we could feel the sexual energy between us, but we never acted on it. We always kept it friendly —nothing more, nothing less. After high school, if we ran into each other, we'd always stop to chat and exchange numbers if our numbers had changed.

We ran into each other during the holiday season. My dad and I were doing last-minute Christmas shopping. It's funny because my dad was the one who pointed him out to me as we were standing in a line in the food court. He was with Chase, and I couldn't believe my eyes because the last time I saw him, he was a little bit taller than me, and I was still six feet two inches tall. Instead of my head being at his shoulder, it was at his chest. I went over to him. "Hey there, Lance." Turning to Chase, "What's going on, Chase? Thanks for not returning my call." Chase was also my godbrother. His mom was my godmother, and my mom was his.

"Hey, Kayla," Lance said with a smile as he hugged me. "How have you been?" I hope you're coming to Chase's Christmas party later tonight?"

"Chase's Christmas party?" I acted like I didn't know, but I did, and both his mom and my mom told me about it.

"Kayla, don't play. I know our moms told you. But hell, the party is the only reason you are in town." Chase said.

Laughing, "Chase, you said that with such conviction. So yes, I'll be there."

"Don't play," Chase said as he hugged me, trying to play fight.

"Good, so I get to see you again, but you never answered me; how have you been?"

"I'm sorry. I've been good. I live in the city now."

Chase cut me off. "She got the fly-pimped-out bachelorette pad over in midtown with a doorman. You know, Kayla, if you don't call to let her know you are coming over, Kayla won't answer. And now, with a doorman I'm sure she's cool with, he will deny you at the door, knowing she is in her apartment. She is also a few blocks from Times Square and the Avenues of Restaurants. Kayla is living it up.

"Don't listen to him. How are things with you?"

"Everything is good; I can't complain."

I heard my dad calling out to me. "Well, I have to go. I'll see you guys later tonight." I walked off and met back up with my dad. We finished our shopping and headed out. He dropped me back at my mother's house. I ate, relaxed briefly, and then got ready for the party. Lance and I did catch up at the party, and naturally, we exchanged numbers since they had changed. He said he would call, but he never did.

It wasn't until six months later that we saw each other again. This time, I was in a different mall with my mother. She was getting her nails done, and I decided to walk around. As I was headed back to see if she was done, I heard someone call my name. When I turned around, to my surprise, Lance was headed my way. "Hey, Kayla."

"Hey, Lance," I said as we greeted each other with a hug.

"I wasn't sure if it was you, so I had my brother call your name."

"Ha, well, it's me." Then, before I could say anything more, he cut me off.

"Look, I want to apologize for not calling you when I said I would. I had gone out of town the next day."

"You don't owe me any explanation."

"I know, but I wanted to tell you. I didn't want you to think I got your number just because."

"I know your intentions are good." My cell phone started to ring. "Oh, that's my mom; she must be done. Look, it was nice seeing you, but I must go." I kissed him on the cheek and gave him another hug.

"Wait, is this still your number?" He showed me my contact information on his phone.

"Yes, it's still the same."

"Let me get that two-way pager number before you go." I gave him the number and left. I couldn't stop smiling when I got in the car with my mom.

"Why are you so happy?" My mom asked.

"No reason."

"Sure, who did you just see?" She asked.

"Lance."

"That explains it." My mom always liked Lance. "So that must mean you're going to stay for the weekend?"

"Um, I really don't know." My pager started to vibrate. I checked it, and it was Lance asking to see me later. Of course, I said yes. "So it looks like you may have me for the weekend." Once we returned to my mom's house, she and I talked briefly and ate dinner. She took a shower and ended up going out. After my shower, I got comfortable, and my cell phone rang. "Hello."

"What's up? The voice asked.

"Nothing." My heart began to beat extremely fast. It was Lance.

"Can I come over?"

"Yes. You remember where my mom lives?"

"I sure do."

"Ok, so how long before you get here?"

"Open the door."

I walked to the door, and when I opened it, there was Lance. I was greeted by one of the biggest hugs and a kiss on the forehead. I closed the door, and he followed me to what I still call my room. "Make yourself at home." He did just that and lay on the bed. I lay down next to him. We talked for a while about the past and present.

"Can I have a kiss?" He asked.

"Sure." I moved closer to him and kissed him. This wasn't any old kiss; it was a long-awaited kiss. We got deeper and deeper into the kiss. The kiss was nice.

He flipped me over, untied my robe, and kissed my breasts. It felt like he wasn't even touching them, but he was. He held them in each hand and took his time with each one. He then kissed his way down to Kay-Kay. He took long, slow licks as he would suck on her occasionally. Finally, he moved his tongue to the beat of the music playing in the background as my body moved to the singer's voice. Lance was so gentle with me. As he made his way back to my breasts, I could feel that he was hard as he was on top of me. Finally, he rolled over to his back so I could be on top. I began to kiss his neck, making my way down to his chest. As my brother would say, I couldn't believe we were finally about to do the damn thing.

Just as he placed himself inside of me, he went limp. Again, I played with his dick to get it hard, and again, as he went inside of Kay-Kay, he went limp. "Can you taste me, Kayla? It's not that I'm not attracted to you; you make me nervous."

"Tell me anything to get me down there.:

"No, it's true; you know I would never lie to you." I began to kiss my way down to his rod as he was still talking. I placed my mouth over only the head and began to suck. I held him in my hand, relaxed my throat, and took all of him in. "Oh, Kayla." I heard him say. As I had him in my mouth, I licked with my tongue. Up and down I went. I flicked my tongue around the tip when I returned to the head. And with all of him in, I would work my tongue all over his rod. I couldn't believe how big he was. He was a good twelve inches and a Magnum extra-large condom user. Once he was hard enough, I was directed to be on top after putting the condom on. He placed himself inside of me....OH MY!

When we started, I was on top; he flipped me over to be on top. He then crossed my legs and rested them on his chest. So it was like I was sitting Indian-style, but on my back. It was a weird position, but it felt good.

We moved with each other. I pulled Lance in closer to me since I wanted all of him inside me. He wrapped my legs around him and began a long stroke. I was back on top, and I rode him well. When I would come down, he would go up. We were still moving to the music. I kept calling his name. "Lance?"

"What's wrong?" He asked as he held onto my hips, never letting them go.

"Nothing. I'm just in shock." I said as I enjoyed myself.

He flipped me over so that he was back on top. And as he moved in and out, we never took our eyes off each other. Finally, he picked me up and sat me on the dresser. He wrapped one leg around his waist and one foot on the dresser and gave it to me. We then moved back to the bed; he sat with me on top of him. He held onto my hips as I went up and down. This was the first time that I ever made a noise. I moan and make noise, but this dick had my noise level at the max. It was a good thing that my mom wasn't home. He lay me across the bed and entered from behind, and as he gave it to me, I was throwing it back at him.

The session started at about midnight and didn't end until four that morning. It was a nonstop session. At some point, the condom came off because Lance came on my ass and wiped it off when we finished. What a guy! Yes, the condom came off. At what point? I don't know, and he didn't stop to put on another.

When we were done, both of my legs were shaking. We both lay there, not believing what had just taken place. It had taken us nine years to have sex. "What's going on through your mind?" He asked.

"I can't believe this."

"Is that good or bad?"

"It's good. I can't believe it after all this time. I wonder if it would have been like this in high school? Wow." I lay there as he ran his hand over my body.

"You have some good pussy. " Lance said out of the blue.

"Tell me anything."

"It's the truth. Can I ask you a question?"

"Sure, go ahead," I said, getting up to put on a pair of shorts and a T-shirt.

"Are you glad you waited?"

"I honestly don't know. Are you?"

"Yep." He said as he got out of bed to put on his clothes. "Look, I would love to stay, but I must get on the road. When I get back into town, I will call you."

"Sure you will," I said, walking to the door, and when we got outside, we talked for a few more minutes before he left. After that, I went back inside, still in a daze, rolled a blunt, went on the deck, and smoked. When I was done, I headed to my room and went to sleep; however, I did go to sleep with a smile.

The next visit was a good one. Lance called me on my way to my mother's house. We met in front of her house; it was good that she wasn't home and on vacation. Before we went at it, we talked briefly and then started. When we started having sex, we had the radio on, and a new deejay began in his timeslot, which lasted for four hours. When we were finished, the next deejay was about to come on. We finally went to sleep, but I had to get up as soon as I fell asleep. When I got out of the shower, Lance was still asleep.

As I was getting dressed, he woke up and watched me. Lance then got out of bed and hugged me from behind. "We sorta look cute together." He said, looking at us in the mirror.

"Yeah, just a little bit," I said. Lance got dressed as I finished, and we both headed out.

A few weeks later, I was at my mom's house and decided to give him a call, and he came over. We chilled for a minute before I went into the shower. He was supposed to join me, but was on the phone, and I didn't want to wait. He cursed me out, but had no problem putting lotion on my body when I got out.

After sex, we lay naked, discussing the past and where we came from. I discovered we grew up in the same town, but hadn't met until junior high school in a different city. We were both amazed.

Lance's next visit was pleasant. I had just returned from dinner with my mom and felt lovely. I had a few drinks at dinner. We chilled as usual when he arrived, and then it was on. As we were fucking, he slipped out of Kay-Kay and went back in without a problem. We both noticed. "Damn, that was easy," I said to him. Yes, at this point, we weren't using condoms.

"Yeah, it was. You're nice and wet." We both laughed. "Can we try something new?" He asked.

I was skeptical, but I thought, Why not. "What's that?"

"Can I put it in the other hole?" My eyes got big. "I'll take it out if you don't like it."

Little did he know I'd already tried it before; I was shocked that he asked. "Okay." He slowly put his dick in my ass as I was on my stomach. His dick was big, and I thought it would hurt, but it wasn't that bad. I let him stay in there for a while, and once I was ready to stop, he took it out and put it back inside Kay-Kay. It actually felt good in my ass. After we finished, we lay there and talked as Lance went through my two-way pager. Yes, we were just friends with benefits, but I had no problem with him going through my pager. I could have gone through his, but I didn't want to or feel the need to. Honestly, I wasn't that curious about his personal business or extracurricular activities; I should have been, but I wasn't. I saw him when I wanted to see him, and that's all that mattered.

"Guess what?" He said.

"What?"

"I leave later than I'm supposed to." He was going overseas to play basketball and thought he'd be leaving within the next few days. Still, the trip was delayed, giving us a little more time to spend together.

"That's great," I said with a smile. So, naturally, if Lance didn't have a basketball game in the city, I would drive to my mom's house after work so we could continue to fuck.

Before Lance left, I got a package delivered to my mother's house and went there to pick it up. I called him on the way to stop by, and he did stop by. We couldn't do anything because it was that time of the month. We talked with the music in the background as I took out his braids for him. After I finished, we were just so into our conversation, but it had to end since he had to get his hair washed and braided. "I hope that everything goes well and you have a safe trip," I said as I walked him to the door.

"Thanks." He said.

"Well, I guess this is goodbye."

"No, let's just say we'll see each other later. "And that's what we did.

While he was away, we kept in touch through email and chatted online occasionally. When he returned, I was happy to see him, but when we had sex, it wasn't the same. The most disappointing thing was that he didn't last as long as usual. Things between us sexually just weren't the same. But we continued to fuck. Some days, it was good, and other days it was meh.

MR. PLATONIC

Will and Kayla met by chance. Kayla was at her mom's house and had taken a walk to get some ice cream. He just so happened to be in the ice cream shop. He struck up a conversation with her. They got their ice cream and thought they were going their separate ways. Instead, their different ways were in the same direction. One weekend, she spent it at her mother's and had a dream about him. She ran into him the next day on her way to the local coffee shop. Of course, she told him about it because it made her — well, us — curious. She also figured she'd get her rocks off since Lance was out of town. I guess they exchanged numbers, and a few hours later, he called her. She went over to his place later that night. They talked and got to know each other.

A few nights later, while Kayla was visiting her mom, she again ended up at his place and got to compare him to the dream. After they finished watching the Lakers-Kings playoff game, he turned off the television, dimmed the lights, and played some music. They actually slow-danced. She ended up giving him a massage, and he returned the favor. They went to the basement. He sat in a chair and had her straddle him as he finished the massage. He massaged me over her pants. Will then flipped her over so that she was in the chair. He pulled off her pants and panties at the same time. Will then began to lick me. He stuck his tongue inside of me as he licked. After I wanna say ten long, deep licks, he let his tongue wander inside me. It felt pretty good. As soon as Kayla felt that tingle in her spine, he stuck his hard dick inside me. As he fucked me, Kayla made sure that I fucked him back. I gripped his dick, and we heard, "Shit!"

"Are you okay?" Kayla asked.

"Yes." *He pulled out and then came back in with his tongue. He started again with those long, deep strokes. His tongue seemed to go deeper and deeper.*

"Mmmmmmmm, oh."

"Are you okay?" He asked as he stuck his hard dick back inside of me.

"I'm ok. It just feels so good," *Kayla said.* "Oh shit!" *Kayla yelled as he began fucking me. He started off slow but picked up the pace. Finally, he found a speed or tempo where I could cream on his dick.*

"Lay right there, don't move. I'll be back." *He said before walking away. He returned with a warm cloth and kindly wiped and dried me off. He put on Kayla's panties, pants, and shoes. He saw that her legs were still shaking as he helped her up. He ended up carrying her from his house to her mom's house.*

When she returned home, she sat on the porch for a minute, and her cell phone rang. It was Lance. Her heart began to beat fast.

"Hello."

"What's up, Kayla? By chance, are you at your mom's house?

Excited, nervous, and scared at the same damn time. "Yes, I am. Why?"

"I'm coming around the corner right now." And just as he said, a car was creeping around the corner. She could feel her heart beating all over her body.

"Wait, what?" The car stopped in front of her mom's house. She stood up and ran inside the house while still on the phone. She was on a mission to grab her towel from her room and jump into the shower. She had just finished having sex with another guy. Not only did she smell like sex, but she smelled like him. Kayla was shaking. Lance knew how to lock the front door if he was in the car. She just wanted to hurry and get the scents off her body. She then realized that he could tell that she had just had sex. Homegirl was shooketh to the max.

"I'm kidding; I'm still in Miami," *she said as she was in her room looking around at the floor, trying to find her face.* "I just called to say hello; I'll be home soon, and I'm hoping we can get together."

"Okay," she said nervously. "I'll see you then." *They both said goodbye. She grabbed her towel and went straight to the shower.*

Will called her the following day. "Good morning, Kayla."

"Hey, Will, how are you?"

"I just wanted to let you know that I woke up with a smile."

Confused, "Okay."

"That's all. Have a good day, and I'll talk to you later." He hung up.

Later that evening, she returned to his place, where they repeated what they had done the night before. This time, his tongue stayed inside of me longer than the night before. He buried his tongue deep inside of me. Every now and then, he moved his tongue around. Then, he would pull his tongue out to lick me all over. Finally, he inserted two fingers inside me and sucked on my clit. His fingers touched something inside me, and my juices were gushing out the next thing I knew. Oh, this man found my G-spot. Baybe!!!! I've had some squirting orgasms before, but this squirting orgasm took us out. Her body jerked harder than it ever jerked before. Her lower body went numb as her upper body felt too heavy to hold up on her elbows. It was like Kayla's energy and strength flowed out with my juices. It took Kayla a good fifteen minutes to get herself together. Once she was ready, she got up to leave.

"Would you like me to give you a piggyback?"

"No, I'm good. I got it. Besides, I'm headed back into the city and driving. But you can walk me to my car."

"Not a problem; let me grab my slippers." *He put on his slippers and walked her to her car.* "Thank you for letting me just taste you."

"You're welcome." *She said, confused since she really didn't know what to say. Then, starting up her car, she said,* "Well, I will talk to you later and perhaps see you the next time I visit my mother."

"You get home safe."

Kayla returned to her place, showered, and got into bed; she decided to let Will know she had made it home, but he called her before she could call. She accepted the call. "Hello."

"What's up?"

"I was just about to call you to let you know I made it back ok. Is everything ok?"

"I was just sitting here thinking about you."

"And what were you thinking about?" She asked curiously.

"Where do you see yourself in five years?" He asked.

"I honestly don't know. Somewhere happy. I just graduated from college, so I'm trying to adjust. I may want to go to graduate school within the next five years or start a business. But, again, I don't know. Why do you ask?"

"I'm looking for a commitment." *Kayla pulled the phone away from her ear and looked at it when he said that.* "Do you think that you can give me that?"

"Uh, uh.um." *Not only was she stunned by what he said, but she was shocked.*

"Well, if you can't give that to me, then I think we should have a platonic relationship."

"Platonic? Sure, that's doable," *she said before hearing a busy signal.* "So what the fuck just happened?" *She asked herself.*

****OH WOWER****

Will was in his late thirties, approaching forty, and looking to get married. I wasn't there; if I were, he wouldn't have been the one. But let me find out we had marry me pussy.

Will wasn't the only person I fucked with while Lance was away. I also fucked with someone from the gym I went to when I visited my mom, Tristan. His body was the shit!! He was only about five feet eight. He was way shorter than me, but his muscles made up for it. He was cut in all the right places. Had a fantastic chest six-pack, a V-line in the pelvic area, and a set of arms. He was short and fine, with his mocha complexion, for no reason. He flirted with me at the gym, and I flirted back. We went out a few times. Two dates stand out that I'll never forget. First, we went to the movies. When we pulled up, there was a restaurant next door to the theater, and Lance and Chase were having dinner sitting in front of the window. I saw them, but I didn't think they saw me. I also didn't know Lance was in town; he was early. Had I known that, Tristan and I wouldn't have gone out. I'm good at canceling plans when Lance comes into town, especially if I have plans the day he arrives.

About thirty minutes into the movie, I get a text from Lance asking whose kid I was with. I busted out laughing, and we weren't watching a comedy. His following text message was to ensure I got him home before his curfew. Again, I busted out laughing. Yes, after the date, Lance broke my back in.

On our second date, he took me to this restaurant in Times Square, not too far away from my place, but he never made it there. This restaurant slowly spun on the top floor of the Marriott Hotel. You couldn't feel it, at least I couldn't, but you could see through the windows. Someone had taken him there. He kept asking me out to dinner, and I told him it had to be someplace nice, and this is where he chose to take me.

When we got there, it was charming. We were seated, and it wasn't like you could order an appetizer, a meal, and dessert if that's what you wanted. I want to say that the appetizer was extra, but the soup/salad, dinner, and dessert were one price per person. I don't know if he remembered this from when he came with whoever brought him to this restaurant, but he wasn't ready for the bill when it arrived. So he had to call his mother and have her pay over the phone. Had I known he had to do that, I would have offered to pay. The sex was good and worth it, but he didn't ask, and I didn't offer.

We continued to fuck after that. Even though we were just fucking, I like to be given the option of being a sidepiece. But who am I to say, or even think, that when I didn't provide Shawn that option? Please don't make the decision for me. One night, Tristan was over, and his cell phone went off. I thought it was mine; I was high. I read the text messages, and I responded as myself. Meaning I was like, he's at my place, and we just finished fucking, and we've been fucking for three months. When he got out of the shower, the chick and I were done with our conversation on his phone. When I was at work, I called and told him what I had done. Afterward, he took his phone into the bathroom whenever we were together.

Yes, we still continued to fuck. One day, I was smoking and was like, Kayla, stop it; what you're doing isn't right. I was right; it wasn't, but did I really care? At that time, no, but it still wasn't right. I'd cut Tristan off when Lance came into town and return to Tristan when Lance left. It was the perfect situation for me. I assume it was perfect for Tristan since the chick I texted was in Canada. He couldn't travel since he was on parole. Yeah, this mothafucka was on parole. It explained the beefed-up upper body and the absence of lower legs. He was something to do and keep my mind occupied when Lance wasn't in town.

My plan was to focus on myself after the Vaughn Tyler situation, but the way things were going with Lance, that focus went out the door. When he left, I would focus on myself again, but still found someone to fuck. Whenever he came into town, we would stay at my place and fuck, or if he wanted to go away, we'd catch a flight and go on a sex vacation. We were terrific friends with exceptional benefits. Before Lance came into town, he'd let me know when, and we would decide whether to go on a mini vacation or chill in town. He was my Mr. Big, and I was now Carrie, not Samantha. To this day, we are still good friends without exceptional benefits. We speak to each other on birthdays and holidays, but we no longer fuck. We had our moments, and those were moments when I should have left his ass alone and never fuck him again, buuuut...the dick was that good.

Moment #1. He emailed me to say we needed to talk. Unfortunately, we kept missing each other, so we never got a chance to chat. He ended up telling me through email. He told me that I needed to get checked out. He tested positive for an STD. I was surprised but not hurt. A week before his email, I had been to my primary care physician and gynecologist for a physical and for Kay-Kay to be checked out. I was good. I respected the fact that he told me. Most dudes wouldn't have said shit or accused me of giving them the STD. Believe it or not, there was no love lost. I should have been done with him, but I wasn't.

Moment #2. He had come into town and said I would see him later, so I drove to my mom's house. I ended up spending the night. He didn't call or stop by. Three days passed, and I hadn't heard from him, so I contacted him. He said he was standing with his fiancée. OUCH!! Although we were friends with benefits who took trips together, neither of us said we saw or dated anyone else. He was going through my two-way pager, so he knew all my business; in hindsight, I should have gone through his. The time that we spent together, we spent TOGETHER! So when I heard that, I was hurt more as a friend because I thought we were being honest with each other. Had he said, Hey, look, Kay, I met someone and want to be with and/or marry this person. I would have wished him the best. But we were friends with benefits, not dating or working on a relationship. At some point between the flights, I may have caught feelings, but I can honestly say that I was more hurt as a friend than a lover; well, at least that's what I was trying to tell myself.

We didn't speak for a few years after that. Chase lived next to his mother, my godmother, and I was visiting her. As I walked to my car, I heard someone call my name. I knew it was Lance; Chase was going into his mom's house when I left, and I knew better. I picked up the pace and did a fast walk and slow jog to my car, but I couldn't get there fast enough because he caught up to me. We talked for a minute. About what? I have no clue. I remember him asking me if I had the same number, and he said he would call me later. So, I went to my mom's house instead of driving back into the city. He called and came over that night, and we talked about our last conversation. He apologized, and I accepted his apology, and yes, we fucked. He was in the process of getting a divorce. Once his divorce was finalized, we returned to being friends with benefits and traveling together. Do I need to remind you that the dick was just that good? We continued being friends with benefits for a few years until he met someone and told me.

I know I should have hated him, but I didn't. Because we were friends first and always talked, we discussed everything. After the STD situation, most chicks would have been like fuck you, don't ever speak to me. But what he said was logical. And he knew he had this STD, but it was dormant. I'm not making any excuses, but his point was that he was only with me — and only me. I had an apartment in the city, but when he was in town, I commuted from my mom's a lot, and there were times when he and Chase hung out; they stayed at my place, or he stayed. So yes, he was always with me, but what was he doing when he wasn't? I can't call the fiancée situation, but that really hurt me. However, once we talked about it, I was okay. He apologized, I accepted his apology, and we moved on. After his divorce, everything was smooth, but then I got bored. I didn't call as often or ask when he was coming into town, and when I found out he was in town, I stopped making myself readily available.

I was soon introduced to my mom's friend's son, Kevin. Kevin and I got along really well. We were the same age at the time. He may have been a few months older than me. He lived out of state, so it was a getaway when I needed it, including dick. How could I go wrong?

STOP!

Kevin was someone I could always joke around with. He lived in Maryland, so I would visit him occasionally. His parents and my mom were friends, and they introduced us. He and his parents had come into town for a wedding, and I just happened to be at my mom's. We hit it off, exchanged numbers, and would talk for hours. He finally convinced me to visit him in Maryland, and I did. Instead of driving down, I took the train into Maryland. The first time I went to see him, we smoked and fucked. After that, we went out to get something to eat.

The sex wasn't anything to brag about. To me, sexually, Kevin wasn't that good. His dick was long, but it was like a pencil dick. Long and thin, no girth. He claimed to be a professional at eating pussy, but he wasn't.

It wasn't until the second visit that I realized I didn't want to have sex with him again. That was quick. We were in the hotel room, and one thing led to another. They were at it for a while, and it didn't feel like anything. I had already stopped gripping his dick; I couldn't grasp anything because it was thin. Kayla even stopped moving. Then, finally, she looked at him and called his name, "Kevin!"

He was so into it. " Yes, baby."

"Stop." With one quick push, she got him out of me.

"What's wrong? Am I hurting you?" He asked.

She wanted to laugh. "No, not at all. I want you to stop."

"Huh?" He was definitely confused.

"I just need you to stop."

"You need a break?"

"No, I just don't want sex with you."

"What's this all about? He asked, strangely looking at her.

"I just felt that we needed to stop." She rolled over and got underneath the covers. He stood there in complete shock. "What?" She asked, looking back at him.

He looked at her, got dressed, and left. He thought he was doing the right thing by leaving her in the hotel room the next day. Little did he know that Derrick lived in Maryland and was just a phone call away. Derrick picked her up, rocked her world, and returned her to the hotel. I'm sure she was prepared with a lie if he was there when she returned. When she got there, Kevin wasn't there. An hour after she got back, Kevin came. "Did you like being here by yourself today?"

Little did he know. "Yeah, I was able to get some work done." She said with a smile.

"Would you like to explain what happened last night?"

"There's nothing to explain." She started to pack her things. He looked at her and left. When he finally returned the next day, it was time to go to the train station.

On the way to the train station, there was silence. Finally, when they arrived, she said goodbye, headed to the platform, and never looked back. Thank goodness because pencil dicks aren't for me. We usually fuck with someone for a while. I think this was the shortest—no, Matt—but can we really count him? Yes, I will count him; I know Kayla doesn't, but I will. So, Kevin was the second person who hadn't become a regular. He tries to get her to visit, and I will be like bitch remember he got that pencil dick. See, me and her brain work together. Her brain forgets to communicate with me when she gets high, but she looks out if that's what you want to call it. I mean, Matt, Shay, she was just curious or outright out of her mothafuckin mind.

BOX OF 3

I had known Grant for about seven years before Kay-Kay actually stepped in. I met him through my best friend, Tionne, and from that moment, he and I took it from there. Grant was what I like to call deep dark chocolate. He had a hidden body; you could not tell he had a nice body, but it was always covered in mechanic's overalls. However, Grant took care of himself. He was six feet even; I guess his hair was low-cut because he always wore a durag and a baseball cap. He was also a brother on the move. I was actually friends with his ex-girlfriend, Candace. But the thing about that was he tried to hook up with me before I went to college, and I was with Marion at the time. I remember coming home one weekend and seeing him and Candace together. His being with her never stopped him from trying to holla at me. I never told Candace I knew Grant, but I always heard her discuss their relationship. And that relationship was filled with drama. But enough of that, let's get into my encounter with Grant.

Grant worked around the corner from my mom's house, and I would stop to talk to him every time I passed by his job. I took the train from the city to see my mom one day. I walked from the train station to her house and stopped by his job. "Hey, Grant, what's good?" He was outside checking on his car.

"Nothing. How have you been? I haven't seen you around in a minute," he said, showing his pearly whites.

"Well, I live in the city now and only come to my mom's on the weekend and when I have days off during the week."

"Do you really come to see her or be with your man?"

"If that's your way of finding out if I got a man, that's slick. But I really do come to see my mom. I work nine to five and don't get here until seven; by then, I like to eat, shower, talk to my mom, and relax. Besides, I'm single. I haven't met anyone that has piqued my interest or curiosity."

"Alright, then. So, can I come to check you out sometime?"

"How about you give me your number? When I want you to visit me when I'm at my mom's, I'll call you."

"I'm giving you my number, so I expect you to use it." So he gave me his number, and I went on my way.

Every now and then, when I visited my mom, I'd see Grant at his job as I passed by. I'd wave and keep it moving. I'd hear him driving in his loud car by my mom's house. A few months after he gave me his number, I decided to call him. I was high and horny. I scrolled through my contacts until I got to his name and hit talk. "Hey, Grant, this is Kayla. What's up?"

"Nothing; I just got back from Miami. What's up?"

"I'm at my mom's, and I was thinking about you, so I decided to give you a call."

"Three months later?"

"Hey, I could have called someone else, and it's never too late to do just that," I said sarcastically, but I meant it.

Laughing, "You are hilarious, you know that?"

"Are you coming or not? I said, getting straight to the point.

"Let me shower, and I'll call you when I'm on my way." "Sounds like a plan." I hung up and took a nap. When I woke up, I showered and straightened up the room. As I was finishing up, my cell phone started to ring. "Hello."

"I'm on my way. Can I bring you anything?"

"Just you."

"I should be there in twenty minutes."

"See you then." Twenty minutes after that phone call, Grant was at the door. I wore shorts, a tank top, and no bra. "Hey there, come on in."

"Damn, Kayla."

"What's wrong?" I asked, confused.

"Your chest always looks right with or without a bra."

Laughing. "I guess I should say thank you, but I won't." We laughed. "Come follow me." He followed me to my bedroom. "I'll be right back. Can I get you a Heineken?"

"Yes, please." So Kayla went to grab him a beer, two shot glasses, and her bottle of tequila out of the freezer.

"Would you like a shot?"

"No, the beer is good."

"Well, it's after seven, so I must take my daily shot. Are you sure you don't want one?"

"I'll have one just so you don't feel lonely.

"Even if you weren't here, I'd still be taking a shot." She poured their shots. She handed him his and downed hers before he drank his. Then, she poured herself another shot. "Are you ready?"

"Yes." They touched glasses and downed their shots. Then, after a brief conversation, it was on.

Grant leaned into Kayla and kissed her on her neck as he played with her breasts. He took off his shirt and hers. Grant kissed and licked her melons, making his way down to me. He pulled out a condom from his pants pocket. He put it on and entered. Oh my! When he got inside me, he responded, "Damn, Kayla!"

"What's wrong?"

"Not a damn thing; you just feel so good."

"Thank you." *He started off slow and gradually picked up the pace. He kept at it, and it felt good. Both Kayla and I were surprised.* "Shit, Grant, this feels good."

"You're right about that." He was picking up the pace. "Oh my."

"Oh shit, oh, Grant!"

"Oh my..oh my..oh my...oh Kayla..oh Kayla."

"Oh, Grant, keep it right there."

"Oh my..oh my...Kayla shit..oh Kayla."

"Yes, Grant..right there..oh like that..oh oh oh oh oh shit, oh...I'm about to cum."

"Oh my..oh my...Kayla..oh Kayla."

"Yes..yes..yes...Grant..yes..oh." *It was like a splashing waterfall when I came. Grant surprised the shit out of both of us. I don't think Kay or myself was prepared for what happened next.* Grant took off the condom and grabbed his jeans. I thought, Oh, he is a smart one. Get your shit, get dressed, and bounce. I was wrong. He went into his pocket, grabbed another condom, and put it on. He entered again, but this time he picked me up. I wrapped my legs around his waist and my arms tightly around his neck as he held me by the hips, controlling the motions. We were like this for fifteen minutes before he lay on the bed, and I was on top. I rode him like a professional. "Oh, Grant."

"Damn, Kayla, you got some good pussy."

Here's where I get cocky, "What's my name?"

"Kayla."

"Louder."

"Kayla!"

"Louder." Thank goodness my mom wasn't here, because he was louder than a Loud House.

"KAYLA! Oh my god..oh my god...Kayla...Kayla..oh shit, yes, ride it."

"Like this?"

"Just like that."

"Oh, Grant, grab my ass." He grabbed my cheeks and squeezed them before spanking them. "Oh yes..oh..oh yes." "I don't want to cum yet. Oh shit, Kayla." He flipped me over and entered from behind. I kept throwing it back at him as he gave it to me. "Oh, Kayla...oh, Kayla.."

Together, we came. When Grant lay down beside me, he went right to sleep. I got up, threw on some clothes, grabbed a cigarette from Grant's pack, and headed downstairs. I grabbed a beer from the refrigerator, went on the deck, and lit up. It was rare that I had sex with someone and smoked a cigarette. I usually smoked a blunt, but tahnight. I couldn't believe how good the sex was. Shit, Candace was getting this when they were together? After finishing the beer and a cigarette, I returned inside and returned to my room. Grant hadn't moved from where I had left him.

I took off my clothes and got back into bed. It was hard for me to sleep since I discovered that I genuinely enjoy sleeping alone. Since the sex was that good, I thought I'd let Grant stay until the morning. But then again, I wanted to sleep, and I'd be damn if someone made me sleep in a different room. He must have been reading my mind or feeling my vibe because he woke up. He went for his jeans and pulled out another condom. Damn! It was like after his quick naps, he was ready to go like he didn't have sex, and I know he came after each time. I enjoyed the sex, but the way he moaned out loud, or just the way he called my name was annoying at this point. Was I over it and really ready for him to go? I think I was because I wanted it to be over quickly.

I think he felt my please be done and go home vibe. After this last round, he put on his clothes and left. When I returned to my bedroom, I turned on the light, looked in the garbage, and saw the empty box of condoms; there were three wrappers and the used condoms. I shook my head. I went to my dresser drawer, grabbed some weed and a backwood, and rolled up. I returned downstairs, grabbed another beer, and went on the deck. As I sat there and smoked, I was still in shock. But I kept laughing; there was something about him, and how he said, "Oh my god," like he was shocked and excited. It was funny and annoying to me at the same time.

That was the only time that Grant and I fucked. I would have loved to fuck him several times, but it never happened. We'd get together and smoke, but never spoke about our hook-up, but there was something about how he looked at me and smiled whenever we smoked or saw each other.

I needed a change of scenery because I wasn't sure if I was ready to return to school and work on my Master's degree, get back to work, or start a business. Although I had enough money to travel and keep my apartment, I couldn't focus. I had been out of school and working for three years, but was agitated. Sometimes, I lived my Sex and the City Samantha life but felt I was missing something. Was I missing love? Did I want love? I spoke to my parents separately, and they agreed with my decision. My mom suggested I visit Kim in Atlanta, but Kim had moved. But my dad had family there, so I did that; I went to see my uncle, my dad's brother, and his wife, my aunt, and my cousin. My cousin, Cali, and I were exactly six months apart and close, just like our fathers. My aunt was thrilled that I was coming to Atlanta. I stayed with Kim every time I went to visit them for a day. While I was there this time around, I met Ryan and Barry.

WORK

Kayla had three drinks in her system when she saw Ryan. His smile made me wet. When she spotted him, he was talking to someone; she did a triple-take. She thought she'd go over and say something to him when he was done talking. Eventually, he finished and headed toward her, but he was stopped again. She got up from her seat, stood beside him, and waited for him to finish his conversation. When he was done, she grabbed his hand before he could walk away. "Hi, my name is Kayla."

"I'm Ryan. You sound like you're from up North."

"Yes, I'm from New York. I saw you earlier talking to someone, and I like what I see, and that's why I'm over here talking to you. So, how are you tonight?"

"I'm fine. How about yourself?"

"I'm good; I'm here in Atlanta visiting family."

"How do you like it so far?"

"Well, this is my first full week here, but I like it so far. So, are you from here?"

"I am. How long will you be here?"

"Long enough to get to know you," she laughed. "I don't know, but I'll be here for a minute."

Smiling, "Okay then, can I buy you a drink?"

"I'll take bottled water, please."

"I mean a drink."

"You asked me if you could buy me a drink, and I told you I would like bottled water. When is water not a drink? I've had enough to drink. I need to sober up." He went to get her water and returned. "So, can I get your number?"

He looked at her, shocked. "Sure. Let me get your phone. She handed him her phone, he entered his number, and then handed it back to her. She called his number.

"And now you have my number." She said, pointing to his phone. "Thanks for the drink." She walked to the dance floor, and he stood there for a minute, watching her dance and watching him.

They spoke on the phone a few times before seeing each other again. She wore a skirt and a tank top when she visited his place. Which was ten minutes away from her uncle and aunt's house. They were sitting on the couch, talking, joking, and laughing when she arrived. He would pull her hair behind her ear whenever it got in her face. When she went to lean on the arm of the couch, he dragged her in his direction so she could lean on him. As she lay on him, he rubbed her arm. He was a gentleman; after a little more conversation, she left. He walked her to the car and gave her a hug. "I'm getting weak," he said to her.

"Why is that?" She asked as she tilted her head and bit her bottom lip.

"You're a sexy woman. I told you I want to take my time with you, but I don't think I can."

"Is that right?" She asked.

"Yes, that's right. Can I see you tomorrow?"

"Sure, I have errands; you can see me before or after."

"How about before and after?"

"Okay, so I'll call you when I get up, and we'll take it from there." She gave him another hug and got into the car. He closed the door, and she dove off."

It was nine in the morning when she heard her cell phone ringing. She looked at it and saw it was Ryan. "Hey Ryan, what's up?"

"Were you asleep?"

"I was, but it's ok; I need to get up anyway. So, again, what's up?"

"I thought maybe we could meet for breakfast, then I could go with you while you run your errands. Kinda be your guide to help you out a little bit."

"That would be nice. Let me jump in the shower, and I'll call you when I'm done and on my way out the door."

"I'll wait for your call," She closed her phone, straightened up her room, picked out something to wear, and prepared to get ready. When she called Ryan, they agreed to meet at the diner around the corner from his place. Ryan was six feet four inches tall, average built, had a mocha complexion, and was an ARMY man. He had a goatee and a neat mini afro. *His smile was peaceful and beautiful, and his southern accent wasn't too heavy, turning Kayla and me on. He was waiting for her when she pulled into the parking lot. He approached the car after she parked. "Hey there,"* he said, opening the car door.

"Hey Ryan, how are you?" She asked as she got out of the car and was greeted with a hug.

"I'm good. Are you hungry?"

"It might look like I don't eat, but I do. But to answer your question, I'm always hungry." They headed into the diner and were immediately seated. "It's nice of you to want to accompany me while I run errands today. Thank you in advance."

"No problem, I didn't have anything to do today since I'm off, so I figured, why not spend some time with you and get to know you more?"

"Again, thank you. I'm ready to order, are you?"

"Yep." He flagged down the waitress, and they ordered. "So, what do you have to do today?"

"Well, I have to go to the post office, then I need to get a few personal effects, and after that, I was going to get lost."

"There's a post office a few blocks down. We can go to Perimeter Mall and then get lost, and I'll help you when you need or want my help."

"That sounds like a plan." After they finished their meal, she followed him home to drop off his car. They went to the post office and the mall, where she didn't have to come out of her pocket. She got her personal effects and a few tops, which he purchased. She told him that he didn't have to, but he insisted. After leaving the mall, Ryan navigated as she drove around to get familiar with the neighborhood. There were only a few strip malls and some hotels around. The highway was a hop, skip, and a jump away, no matter where she seemed to be. Before it got dark, they headed back to Ryan's place. "You live by yourself?" She asked as she parked the car.

"Did you see anybody when you were here the other day?"

"Touche. However, they could have been out. So again, do you live by yourself?"

"As I told you before, I was engaged; now I'm not; I'm single, living all alone. Are you hungry?"

"I was just asking. Am I hungry? Yes, are you cooking, or are we ordering out?"

"Whichever you want, I have some chicken already cleaned and seasoned."

"What are you going to make with the chicken?" She asked as they got out of the car.

"I can make some collard greens, heat up the mac and cheese I made yesterday, and cut up some yams quickly."

"A Sunday meal on a Monday. That sounds good."

"You can make yourself at home, and I'll go fix us dinner, or you can keep me company as I cook."

"I'll keep you company. Make sure you can cook and not heat up some precooked food."

Laughing, "You're funny. Want a glass of wine?"

"Yes, please." She said as she pulled out a chair at the counter. "So why aren't you engaged anymore? What happened?"

"She cheated on me, and I found out."

"Oh wow, were you not putting it on her?"

"You can let me know."

She clutches her imaginary pearls and laughs, "What do you mean by that?"

Laughing, "You know what I mean."

"You're funny," she sipped her wine and mumbled, "I hope sooner rather than later."

"Speak up."

Shouting, "I said I hope to find out sooner than later. Was that loud enough for you?"

"Shit, you can find out now if you want."

"But you're cooking."

"I don't have to."

"Well, let's get to it."

Ryan walked from behind the counter to her face. He picked her up from the chair and placed her on the counter. He lifted her skirt and pulled her thong to the side. "Oh, you're nice and clean."

"I like to take care of her and keep her well-groomed."

"I like it like that." He said before he took a lick. "And you taste good as well." *He took another lick before burying his tongue inside of me. He licked and sucked. He then stuck a finger inside of me as he licked. Why must these men stick their fingers inside of me? He grabbed Kayla's hands, placed them on his head, and pulled us in closer so there was no space. My girl Kayla began to fuck the shit out of his face as she held on to his head. He continued to lick and suck while using his fingers.* "Mmhmm." *He said with me now in his mouth.* "Mmmhmm."

"Ffffffffuck!" Kayla shouted. Her body was starting to shake. Then he stopped. "Why'd you stop?"

"Because we're taking this to the bedroom. I need you, well, us to get into this."

"I can't move."

"Don't worry, I got you." He picked her up, carried her to the bedroom, and dropped her on the bed. "Take off the rest of your clothes."

"Demanding. Sexy." She said, and then she began to take off her clothes. "Hush," He aggressively said as he got on top of her and kissed her. He bit her bottom lip, making his way to her neck and then her breasts. Ryan took one in each hand, squeezed them, and teased the nipples with his tongue until they were hard. He sucked harder. Ryan made his way back to me, licking and sucking. He stuck his finger inside of me again as he sucked on me. Her entire body went numb. He fingered me faster and sucked harder. He stopped sucking and continued to finger me; the next thing I knew, there was a waterfall. "That's what I'm talking about. Now you're ready." He said.

"Ready for what?" I asked, out of breath.

"Don't tell me you're about to tap out."

"Tap what? I ain't never tapped out." In her head, except with Kevin, and that's because it wasn't good and didn't feel good. "How about you lie down and let me do what I do."

"Oh, you bossy?"

"I'm really not. Now, lie down." He did as I said, and I got between his legs and stroked his dick. "Nice."

"Thank you."

I began to suck on the tip before I started to savor all of him. As I sucked, I jerked. I sucked the tip as if I were sucking a lollipop. I began to feel his dick getting hard as I sucked. Then, I stopped, got up, squatted over him, and slid Kay-Kay down on his erect appendage. Up and down, I went and gyrated my hips as I straddled him. As I sat on his hard cock, I moved my hips around in a circular motion, adding the up and down, and I could hear that he was enjoying himself. "You like that?"

"Mmmhmmmmm," he moaned. I got up but did not let him come out of her; I turned around, grabbed his ankles, and began to bounce off his dick. I started winding my hips. Just as I did that, he grabbed my hips and shook me up and down on his dick. "What are you doing?" I asked.

"Nothing."

Looking back at him, "Doesn't feel like nothing." I grabbed his hands and spun around. I leaned in to kiss him, but went for his ear and nibbled on it. Then, grinding on him, "How does that feel?" I asked him. "You like that?"

"Feels good, real good," He said.

I pushed myself up with him inside Kay-Kay, still riding and gyrating. He leaned up and started sucking on my breasts. "Suck harder," I whispered in his ear, and he did. "Harder." He complied. "Just like that. Don't stop." I said as I gyrated my hips faster. It was turning me on and making Kay-Kay wetter.

"Oh shit." He said as he stopped sucking on my breasts.

"Don't stop!"

"I'm about to cum." He said.

"If you cum, can you get it back up?"

"With your help, yes."

"I got you; now go back to sucking." I put my tittie back in his mouth. He sucked on my breast as I rode him until we both came.

"Shit!"

"What's the matter?" I asked.

"Nothing at all." He grabbed a towel and wiped off his dick. I scooted between his legs and sucked him until he was hard again. Once, he was hard and wasn't going limp. I slid back down on his dick and began up-and-down movements in reverse cowgirl style.

"You don't like looking me in the eyes?"

"First of all, we are not making love; we are just fucking, so there's no need to look you in the eyes."

"You're right; you are absolutely right." He leaned up and pushed me over so I was on my knees; he grabbed my hips and slammed me back on his dick. I managed to spread one leg out to the side. He held on to my hips with one hand and used the other hand to play with Kay-Kay as he fucked me from behind. "How do you like that?"

"Oh shit, this feels good." He pounded me out until we both came. Then, he pulled out and came all over my ass. But he was a gentleman; he got a warm washcloth and wiped my ass. "Can I get a pair of shorts?"

"Sure." He went into his closet and grabbed a pair for him and me. We got comfortable and lay on the bed. He turned on the television. We held each other as we watched television. "Does that answer your question?"

Confused, "What question?"

"Me putting it on my ex-fiancée?"

"Oh shit, it answers my own question ."

"What's that?"

"Can you fuck as good as you look? And yes, you can."

Laughing, "Can I ask you a question?"

Hesitant, "Yes."

"Why do you say it like that?"

"Yes, Ryan, you can ask me a question. What would you like to know?"

"Well, I have a couple."

"And you asked me if you could ask me a question. Meaning one, so I suggest you pick the question to which you want to know the answer."

"Do you ever submit sexually?"

"What do you mean?"

"Do you ever let a man have control?"

"Not when I'm on top unless you do what you did."

"Okay."

"That's your question?"

"Yes, it was."

"Whatever." He held me tighter, and when I woke up, it was morning. When I looked around, he wasn't there. I could hear the shower. I walked over to the bathroom door and opened it. "Can I join you?"

"Only if you do what I say."

I walked in and joined him in the shower. "So, what do I have to do?"

"Turn around and bend over."

I did, "Okay, now what?"

"Hush, and don't say anything unless it feels good." Ryan entered from behind. His southern accent did something to me; it woke Kay-Kay up. I moaned as he pounded me from behind because it felt good. I think we fucked until we were both wrinkled; after we were done fucking we did wash. Then, I got another pair of shorts and one of his tank tops and got ready to leave.

"Can I see you after I get off work?" He asked as I was heading out.

"If you want to."

"Well, I do, and I want you to do what you did last night."

Laughing, "What did I do last night?"

"You took those backshots like a champion and rode this dick like no other. Oh, and I can't forget about that mouth. So I want a repeat of all that."

"You got it. Oh, and you still owe me dinner."

"Oh, you put that work in last night, and this morning, so you got it. I'll call you on my lunch, and we'll figure it out later."

"Talk to you then." I got in the car and drove off.

While I was in Atlanta, Ryan and I continued to fuck with each other. We fucked about three or four times a week. He'd come to see me on his lunch break and have me for lunch, or I'd go to his house when he got off work. He'd always have dinner cooked. This guy could really cook. Here's the funny thing: the first night I stayed over, I had this dream: a lady came to me and told me to take care of her son. I asked her who her son was, and she said, "Ryan." I said okay. I'd try. A few weeks after that dream, I asked Ryan about his mom and why he never spoke about her. As it turns out, she passed. Weird...Didn't bother to tell him about the dream.

HOW MANY TIMES?

Now, Barry was a close friend of the family. Oh, my bad, I'm still in Atlanta. I was thinking about relocating there at this point. Anyway, Barry would come over just about every weekend. This particular weekend, he came over, and for some reason, this was the first time that I looked at him, and even though he was on the short side, he was still attractive. Not my type —tall or athletic. He was about five feet eight or nine inches tall, with light skin, a round face, and a goatee. That damn Southern accent just did something to me. Okay, let's go back to how this encounter happened. My uncle was having a little get-together this weekend, as they did every weekend, and Barry was over as usual. We ran out of wine coolers, and Walgreens was open and sold them. Barry volunteered to go, and he asked me to ride with him. I did. The whole night, he kept making slick comments to me. He would say, "Just because you're tall doesn't mean I can't take you down". Whatever Barry. He also commented on how long my legs were. It was hot, and I had on shorts. I let his comments slide until we got in his car. "Barry, you talk a lot of shit for a short guy." I knew that would strike a nerve.

"And I can back all my shit-talking up."

"I betcha you can't."

"I bet the fuck I can and will."

"You scared of all this?"

"I ain't scared of shit." He confidently said.

"Put your money where your mouth is."

"Little girl, trust me when I say you are not ready for this."

"Whenever you're ready, Barry and I'm not playing games, let me know." Damn, I was sounding like a guy. "And who are you calling a little girl, Shorty?" We arrived at Walgreens, got the wine coolers, and returned. When we got back, Barry started his shit-talking again. We ended up exchanging numbers that night before he left. Barry called me on his way home, and we talked. Barry had three kids and was in a marriage he was trying to get out of. So Barry called me every day, and we saw each other every Saturday —or, shall I say, we saw each other the days I didn't see Ryan.

The day finally came when Barry stopped bullshitting. He got us a hotel room. We checked in, and I was ready. We got comfortable on the bed. I had my head on his shoulder, put my hands down his pants, and he kept stopping me. I'm thinking, who's the female and male right now? I was making all the moves, and he was fighting me off like a bitch, "Barry, why are we here?"

"So we can spend some time together." "Shit, we could have done that at my uncle's house. My cousin was there; all three of us could have hung out. We've talked on the phone long enough and have spent enough time together. So what's the problem?"

"Nothing."

"So why are you playing games? I told you you couldn't handle me."

"Can I have a kiss?"

"For what? There's no need for us to kiss." He looked at me crazily. I know what I said, and it sounded fucked up. So, I kissed him on his cheek and neck as I put my hands down his pants. As I kissed him on his neck, he relaxed as I played with his dick. Once I got it hard, I pulled his pants down, pulled up my skirt, and slid my panties to the side. Then, I slid down on his dick and slowly rode him. He wasn't that big, and he wasn't that small. I needed to ensure that I rode him slowly because he seemed like once he busted a nut, and I kept going, I'd be humping him. So, with his help, I sped up. He held and helped me go up and down as I squatted over him. But as I sped up, I could hear him, "Oh shit, baby, I'm about to cum, and I'm not ready."

"So don't cum."

Before he could say anything, he stopped me and held me in mid-air. He came, and he was still hard. There was tissue by the bed. He used them to wipe himself off, and thank goodness he was still hard. I slid back down, and he pulled out with quickness. Within seconds, he came again. "Oh shit. Did I come twice back-to-back?"

"Apparently so. Has that ever happened before?"

"No. I must admit you do have some good pussy. Whew!"

Did he say, "Whew?" What the fuck for? Cause he didn't do anything. "You need some time?"

"I'm done; I can't go anymore."

I looked at him and shook my head.

After that episode, there wasn't another episode. I stuck with Ryan; at least I knew he could go rounds and make me not only orgasm, but he could make me squirt and cum all night. I knew for a fact that Ryan could handle me. Every time Barry and I spoke after, I made him come twice, equivalent to a female having multiple orgasms. He'd always start the conversation by asking, "Baby, how many times?"

When I left Atlanta, I didn't tell him I was going. So when he called me and asked where I was, I told him I was in my apartment in New York.

Ryan was naturally a sweet person with whom I am still in contact. His son is actually a few months older than my daughter. Barry, on the other hand, we don't speak. Well, we've talked a few times, and every time he asks when I'm coming back down or if I miss him, he brings up his multiple orgasms. Once he went there, I'd cut the conversation short.

On my last day in Atlanta, I called Ryan and told him I was leaving the next day. After he got off work, he went home, cooked, and then came to pick me up, and I spent the night with him. He didn't speak to me or fix my plate like usual. We ate in silence. I cleaned the kitchen for the last time and joined him on the couch. He was laid out on it, and I sat on the end where there was little space. He got up, pulled me between his legs so my back was on his chest, and held me from behind. We watched a movie like that in silence. It was pretty awkward because we always talked to each other. Our communication was exceptional; we could talk, joke, and agree to disagree. After the movie, he gently pushed me off him, got up, grabbed my hand, and led me to the bedroom. He told me to lie down; he got on top of me, passionately kissed me, went to my breasts, and further down to Kay-Kay. He inserted himself inside of her and made love to me. That was a fantastic night and send-off. When we were done, I dressed, and he took me back to my uncle's. He actually, he took me to the airport the next day. On the way to the airport, he told me he was upset that I was leaving and that I had told him the day before. I apologized and asked him to accept my apology. I wasn't planning to stay longer than three months, and I thought I told him. It took him a few weeks to accept my apology, but at least we were on good terms.

When I returned to New York and got to my apartment, I was happy to be back, and at least my mind was clear. I was mentally ready to start the next chapter. Sexually, up until his point, I discovered that I had marry-me pussy; I could be friends with a good friend after being in a sexual relationship with him; it's all about being able to have uncomfortable conversations. I learned that I often have male qualities when it comes to sex. Sometimes, I'm the male and not the female. I also get bored rather quickly; the excitement doesn't last long. I didn't know what was in store, but I was up for whatever happened.

THE LICKER

I've known Donald ever since I was a little girl. He is friends with my brother, who is a few years older than him, and my brother is ten years older than me. I don't remember, but Donald might be between ten and fifteen years older than me, or just in his late forties or early fifties, and on his second marriage. He actually looked his age. He had stopped by to see my mom; naturally, I was at her house. It was winter, and my mom had the heat on blast, so I was in a tank top with a built-in bra, so my titties were sitting up and were perky, and some booty shorts. I entered the kitchen, and they sat at the counter talking. Before I could turn around and return upstairs to put on a pair of sweatpants, Donald grabbed and hugged me and wouldn't let go."Heyyyy Kayla, how are you? How is city life treating you?"

"Hi, Donald. I'm good, and actually, city life is just fine. How are you?"

"I'm good. I haven't seen you in such a long time."

"Yes, I know. The last time I saw you was in high school. I am now a college graduate and about to start graduate school."

"So, where is your boyfriend?"

"Where's your wife?" I said in my head, well, at least that's what I thought. "I don't have one. Mommy, are you cooking?"

"Are you hungry?"

"Yes, but if you aren't cooking anything, I'll pick up something on my way home."

"Good, because I don't feel like cooking."

"Are you ladies hungry? I'll pay if you have something delivered." Turning to Kayla, "My wife should be at home."

"Does Chinese sound good?" My mom asked.

"That sounds fine. I'll have my normal Shrimp Egg Foo Young with Shrimp Fried rice, both with an extra dollar of shrimp."

"Donald, do you want something?" My mom asked as she was calling to place the order."

"No, thank you. But, unfortunately, I'm not in the mood for Chinese." He said, looking at me.

"So, what are you in the mood for?" I asked.

"What I want isn't on the Chinese menu." He said, smiling at me.

"Well, what are you in the mood for?" I asked curiously.

Smirking, "I'll tell you later."

"Well, alrighty then. Mommy, let me know when the food is here. I'm going back to my room."

"I don't know why you keep calling it your room. That's my other closet, and your brother's room is my shoe closet." She said, laughing.

"You are absolutely right. It is your closet, but when I'm here, it's my room."

"Where's the bathroom?" Donald asked.

"There's one downstairs and one right up these stairs on the right."

"Where are you going, Kayla?"

"Upstairs to my mom's closet room."

"Ok, show me that bathroom."

"The bathroom down here is much closer; it's just right there," I said, pointing toward it.

"No, the one upstairs will do."

"Whatever, follow me." I showed him to the bathroom, went to my room, and shut the door. Two minutes later, I heard a knock at the door. "Come in." It was Donald.

"Kayla, what's your number?"

"Is there a reason why you need my number?"

"Just in case I'm in the city and it's late, I have a place to crash."

"Who said you can crash at my place? That's bold of you to assume that I'm going to say it's ok, or even if I'm up, who's to say I will answer my phone?"

"Damn, you are rude, just like your brother."

"We get it from our mother."

"Are you going to give me your number or not?"

"I guess you can have it, but don't be calling me all willy-nilly."

"I won't."

I gave him my number, and he went back downstairs. Fifteen minutes later, my mom called me to come downstairs.

"Yes."

"Food is here."

"Thanks, Donald."

"You ladies are welcome."

"Kayla, before I forget, I'm going away in two weeks, and I know you are on vacation that same week. I'm going to need you to get my mail if you can. I'm also expecting a package. So, can you stay here that week?"

"Sure."

"Okay, ladies, I'm leaving. I have to get back to work."

"Thanks for dinner." My mom said.

"I'll walk you to the door." When we got there, he turned around and gave me a hug. This time, it was a little different from the last hug. He moaned a little, hugged me waaay too tight, and rubbed his dick against me. "It was nice seeing you, and thank you again for dinner.

"No problem, and it was good seeing you. I'm going to give you a call one day this week."

"Okay, but how about you call me now so I can lock in your number. I don't pick up calls from numbers I don't know." He pulled out his phone and called me. "Great, I'll lock it in when I return upstairs." I returned to the kitchen, finished my food, and talked to my mom. "When did he get here?"

"You must have been asleep when he came here. He stops by once a week, actually."

"Really? Why?"

"I ran into him a few months ago, and we talked for a good hour, and he said he'd come by to check on me since you and your brother moved out. And he's been doing it every week since then."

"That's nice of him. Well, I hate to eat and run, but it's not like you cooked, so there's nothing to clean, so I'm going to head home."

"No problem; I'll talk to you or see you tomorrow since you're always here."

"Funny. I will call you tomorrow." I went upstairs and got my pocketbook and phone. I saw the missed call and saved it under Donald's name, but I called to make sure it was him before doing so. "Donald?"

"Hey, Kayla! What's going on?"

Why was he talking to me like he didn't see me? "I'm fine. Just making sure this was you. It is, so I will speak to you another time."

"Wait before you hang up."

"Yeah, what's up?"

"You look good."

"Uh, thank you." That caught me off guard, "Hold on for a second." Then, as I walked past my mom, I said, "Mommy, I'll speak to you tomorrow." I gave her a hug and a kiss goodbye, then headed to my car. I plugged in my earpiece to continue my conversation with Donald. "Donald, are you there?"

"Yes, I am."

"Sorry about that. I was leaving, and now I'm getting situated in my car."

"No problem. So when will I be able to see you again?"

"I don't know. Maybe the next time I come up. I usually come up once a week."

"Okay, and I stop by once a week."

"I heard that's really sweet of you."

"So maybe we can meet at my mom's place."

"That's fine. Can I call you later?"

"Sure. Talk to you soon." I ended the call.

The next day, Donald started sending me text messages. He kept complimenting me on how much I'd grown into such a beautiful and sexy young lady. Finally, Donald said he wouldn't mind taking me out to dinner. All the while, I'm thinking, isn't this motherfucker married? But the streets said both he and his wife were creeping. Apparently, neither of them respected their marriage. So why should I? So, after all the compliments and sex talk, I invited him over when my mom left. He was excited as we agreed on a day. On the said day, I decided to do something crazy. We talked about fantasies, and one of his was saving a 'princess.' So I told him that I'd make that fantasy come true.

The day came; I went out to run some errands. When I got to my mother's, I showered and shaved. After my shower, I wrote down clues and placed them in different locations. So he was going on a scavenger hunt, but had to do something and remove a piece of clothing. By the time he got to my room, he was naked, and I handcuffed myself to my bed and was blindfolded. When he got to me, he did the strangest thing. The first thing wasn't so strange; he gave Kay-Kay a few licks. Then, after he kissed me all over my body, he began to lick my freshly shaven armpits. And when I say he licked them, he licked them as if he were licking Kay-Kay. He was between my legs, and I could feel him getting hard. I found this strange, but hey, to each his own. He then placed his penis inside of Kay-Kay and continued to lick my armpits as he fucked me. After about ten minutes, he was done.

"Damn, Kayla, you have some sweet pussy."

"Thank you," I said, rushing to get dressed so he could hurry up and leave, but then I remembered his clothes were scattered throughout the house. So after I got dressed, I went and got his clothes for him and practically threw them at him. I didn't throw them; I tossed them beside him.

"Can we do this again?" He asked.

"Do what, this fantasy thing?"

"No, just have sex in general. Perhaps you can come to my office?"

"Now, there's a fantasy for me." Donald had his own security business. He provided security to the local clubs, apartment complexes, and events. "Sure, just let me know your hours, and maybe I'll surprise you."

"Well, I work nine in the morning to about twelve at night. So you can come literally any time."

Laughing, "You're funny. I will definitely give you a call when I'm coming this way. "When he was done getting dressed, I was ready for him to leave, "You good?"

"Yes."

"Okay, I'll walk you to the door." When we got to the door, he tried to get a kiss, but I went in for a hug.

A few weeks later, I went to his office, and we had office sex. "Hello."

"Hi, how may I help you?"

Going along with the fantasy, "I have an event. I'm going to need a few security guards. I was told that you could help me."

"Yes, come into my office." Pointing to a chair, "Have a seat."

I went behind his desk and sat in his chair; he closed the door, walked over to the desk, and sat in front of me. He pulled down my sweatpants and took one leg out with my thong. He spread my legs apart and began sucking on Kay-Kay. I wished he'd lick her the way that he licked my armpits. But he was doing a pretty good job. I could feel myself about to orgasm right before he stopped. He then stuck his dick inside of me and started pounding me out. The faster he went, the more turned on I got. Or was it that we were in his office, and his partner could come in any minute? We fucked until we heard the door to the office open. His partner shouted his name, and he started fucking me faster. It was feeling good, and Kay-Kay was wet. His partner in the next room turned me on more. Finally, the telephone rang, "Greg, can you get that?" He shouted as he continued to pound me out.

"It's your wife." He shouted back.

I was turned on even more. Shouting back, "I'll call her back." He looked at me, "This is too good to stop, and I'm on the verge of coming."

"Fuck me harder," I said, and he did. "Just like that."

"Like that?" He asked as he went harder and faster.

"Ohh, just like that."

"Oh shit, I'm about to cum."

"Fuck me harder."

"Like that?"

"Yes, just like that." I moaned. "Shit, I'm about to cum." Then, well, at least I thought I was, he stopped. He pulled out and came on my thigh. He grabbed a tissue to wipe the cum off my thigh. He pulled up his pants, I fixed my clothes, and I sat in front of his desk. He sprayed some Lysol. As he was spraying, I noticed that the window was open. It was an excellent thing, it was because it would have smelt like sex, and there wouldn't have been any explanation for the smell.

His partner entered his office and looked at me, "Hello."

"Greg, this is Kayla. Kayla, this is my partner, Greg."

"Hello." He extended his hand out to shake mine. "Well, Donald, thank you for your help; I'll call you if something changes," I said as I was headed out.

"Yes, just call me."

I called him several times and drove from the city to have office sex. The last time we had office sex, his partner almost caught us. It was a close call.

CO-WORKERS

Whenever Dustin saw me, he always had something to say. I always laughed it off and kept it moving. To me, he resembled the wrestler John Cena minus the muscles. For some reason, whenever he had a date or went out and met a woman, he always felt the need to come tell me about it. In particular, I didn't see this conversation coming this one day. When he came into my office, I was working at my desk. Dustin walked in, pulled up a chair, and sat beside me.

"Kayla, how are you today?"

"I'm fine. How are you?"

"I'm good. Do you have a couple of minutes to talk?"

Strangely looking at him, "Yes, is everything ok?"

"Yes, everything is fine. But I can't stop thinking about you."

Shocked, "Excuse me?"

Laughing, "You heard me."

"Nah, no, I didn't. Repeat that one more time." I heard him.

"I can't stop thinking about you. It's to the point where I'm dreaming about you, and you are wrapping your legs around my neck."

Shocked, "Dustin!"

"What? I'm serious."

"I don't know if I should be flattered or offended?"

"Why do you say that?"

"Because of the women you describe that you date. I mean, I had seen one who looked like a recovering meth head, and when I bumped into you and your date one night, she looked shocked that you picked her."

"You do have a point. I want to bust a nut, and when I get to the bar and have a few drinks, let's say I am shocked when we get in good lighting."

"I know I have a point, so should I be flattered or what? Hell, I think I might be an improvement for you."

"You are right; you are an improvement."

"Thank you, I guess. Is there anything else?" I wanted to get back to my work. I had office supplies to order, bills to pay, and a payroll to submit. I was the office manager at the company we worked for.

"Well, would you go out to dinner with me?"

"When?"

"Better yet, how about lunch today?"

"Sure, why not?" I can't believe I said that. He wasn't the first co-worker that I went to eat with. The last guy, Antonio, thought I would give him some ass on the first night. I could have, but I do have morals every now and then. When I started working for the company, he would order and pay for my breakfast. He eventually asked me to dinner, and I went. We had dinner, then went to a co-worker's place, where the weed was delivered and good. White people get the best weed. Anyway, we were smoking, laughing, and having a great time until he asked me to go into the bedroom, where I turned down his advances. After that, the breakfast stopped, and he stopped coming by my office. Oh well.

"Okay, so I'll meet you in the lobby at one since that's when you take your lunch."

"Damn, what time do I get here, and what time do I leave?" I asked him.

"You arrive at eight-thirty and leave at four-thirty or five, depending on the day. So, yes, I watch you."

"Don't do that." And I will meet you in the lobby at one."

We met in the lobby and went for sushi. We had a great conversation, and I discovered Dustin wasn't that bad. He was a nice guy and liked all women, no matter their color, size, or height. After enjoying our sushi, we returned to the office and continued our conversation.

"Kayla, can I ask you a question?"

"Sure."

"What in the hell did you see in Antonio?"

"Huh?"

"Why did you date?" I cut him off mid-sentence.

"First of all, we didn't date; we just went out to dinner, and when I wouldn't fuck him, he stopped buying me breakfast and coming by my office just to talk."

"Damn, no need to bite my head off."

"Did he tell you something different?"

"No, I just saw how he acted towards you, and then he changed after you turned him down." I bet you won't turn me down."

Thank goodness we were in the elevator alone. "You wouldn't know what to do with me."

Laughing, "You wouldn't know what to do with me." He repeated. The elevator doors opened. "Whatever." I walked off and headed to my office. I couldn't stop thinking about Dustin and our conversation. I became curious about this white man who looked like John Cena. Again, he wasn't muscular like him, but I could tell he had a pretty decent body. I managed to get my work done while being curious. I wasn't expecting Dustin to return to my office, but he did and shut the door. "You can knock before coming in, and why did you shut my door?"

"Does it lock?"

"Yes." I heard the door lock, and he walked over to my desk.

"Again, why did you shut my door, and secondly, why did you lock it?" I asked, standing up.

"Just be quiet and go with the flow." He said to me.

"I did." Before I could do anything, he kissed me. That kiss made Kay-Kay wet, and she began to throb. Wrong place to be, throbbing bitch. He moved to my neck as he unbuttoned my shirt. He grabbed my breasts and started to play with my nipples with his thumbs. Next, I felt his mouth on them. He licked and sucked and did that so well that I felt a tingle through my spine. Kay-Kay was open, wet, and throbbing. She was ready. He pushed me onto my desk, unbuttoned my pants, and pulled them down along with my panties. He sat in my chair and pushed me further back to my desk. He began to lick her. I heard him moan as he licked.

"You are sweet." He said in the middle of a lick.

"Shh, and return to what you were doing," I replied. I heard Dustin let out a little laugh, and he went back to licking and sucking on Kay-Kay. My legs were draped over his shoulders as he held onto my hips. I was sitting on my elbow with one hand on his head. I slowly started to fuck his face. I couldn't stop thinking about how this white man was eating my pussy better than some men in my past. Like, how was that possible? I heard him moaning, and that turned me on even more. Then, as my body started to shake, he stopped. He unzipped his pants, pulled out his hard dick, and grabbed it. He brushed the tip up and down my entrance before he slid inside. "Oh shit," I moaned.

"Oh, you're nice, wet, and warm. Just like I like my pussy to be."

"Whatever," I moaned. I must admit it felt good. The harder Dustin tunneled in me, the louder I moaned and thought, Oh, so this is why he closed and locked my door.

"You got some good pussy, and it's super wet."

"So I've been told."

"Well, believe it." Then, he got re-focused and slowed down his stroking, "Damn, you're going to make me nut quick, and I don't want to do that."

"It's okay if you're a minute, man. Your secret is safe with me."

Focused on his strokes, he said, "I need more than a minute. Damn, why does your pussy get to be this good?"

"I don't know, but just keep it like that." His stroking wasn't too fast and not too slow. It was like he was listening to a song and moving to that beat. I felt myself starting to orgasm. "Oh shit, just like that, don't stop." He began to speed up. "No, slow down, return to what you were doing." He stopped, pulled out, and came on me. Dustin then went down and started to fuck me with his tongue. I grabbed his head and fucked his face until I orgasmed. "Shit!"

"I told you I could handle you."

"Yeah, okay," I said, trying to catch my breath.

"Does this white boy have skills?"

I looked around my office.

"What are you looking for? I asked you a question."

"You aight." He was more than aight. I tried to get up from my desk, but my legs were shaky. I fixed myself so I could sit at my desk. "You can get out of my chair."

"I'm not going to lie, but I'm a little weak."

"Take your weak ass to the other chair." I wanted to sit in my chair to relax and gather a bit. Once I gained my composure, I grabbed the Lysol from my desk and sprayed my office.

"Oh, you have office sex on the regular?"

"Why would you ask that?"

"The Lysol."

"No, sometimes I eat in my office and don't want my office to smell like my lunch. Are you good?"

"Yes, why?"

"Because I want to leave, and I'd appreciate it if you unlock and open my door."

"There's nobody here."

"That's what you think, but the bosses don't leave until seven."

"Oh, damn."

"No, oh damn, get up, unlock my door, open it, and leave so I can leave."

"This was nice; I hope that we can do this again. I will see you tomorrow." He said as he got up to leave my office.

"Yes, see you tomorrow," I said as I gathered my things to leave. I didn't want to be caught by my bosses because I wouldn't be leaving until seven, and it was already a little after five. After putting on my jacket, I grabbed my pocketbook and jogged to the elevator. I really didn't want the bosses to see me.

As I reached the elevator, I pushed the button, and the doors opened, "Yes!" I quietly screamed. When I got to the lobby, there was Dustin.

"Can I give you a ride home?"

Politely, "No."

"You sure?"

"Yes, I drove today, but thanks." So, I proceeded to the garage and waited for the attendant to bring my car. One perk was free parking courtesy of my job, so I didn't have to take the train and worry about parking. While waiting for my car, my cell phone rang; it was Dustin. "Yes, Dustin?"

"I want to fuck you some more. Can I come over to your place?"

"I'm not there yet; I'm still waiting for my car."

"That's not a no, so I will meet you at your place."

Before I could say anything, the call ended. All I could do was look at my phone and laugh. Then, when my car was in front of me, I tipped the attendant, got in, and headed home, and sure enough, Dustin was outside the building. I parked in the lot and walked to my building. "Were you waiting long?" I asked as I got closer.

"No, it took me like ten minutes to find parking."

"That's good," I said as we headed into my building.

"I was going to call you tonight, but I couldn't wait."

"Why couldn't you wait?"

"Because I want some more of that pussy now. I only need five minutes to recover after the first, but if the pussy is good. And you, my lady, have some good pussy."

"Alrighty then." We got on the elevator and rode to my apartment. "Make yourself comfortable; I want to shower quickly." I went into my bedroom, undressed, and took a shower. I heard a knock on my bedroom door when I exited the bathroom. "It's open."

Walking into my room, I don't know why you showered because it didn't matter."

"Because I wanted to. Can I ask you something?

"Sure."

"How many black women have you been with?"

"You are the first. How many white men have you been with?"

"Could have been two, but only the one in college."

"What happened, if you don't mind me asking?"

"The one in college, a bunch of girls were after him, I think because he looked like Jon B. He and I hung out with the same people, and we hit it off, and we started fucking around. The other guy was from home, and we were cool. One night, a bunch of us were hanging out, and it was late; he invited me over, and I thought we would have sex because we were flirting, but that wasn't the case. We go inside his house and then to his room. We were lying on the bed and started talking. We both fell asleep. I felt movement on the bed; his back was to me when I opened my eyes. I lifted my head up and discovered that he was jerking off. I was shocked. I put my head down, closed my eyes, and didn't move until he was finished.

Laughing, "What?!"

"Yes. It took me a while to fall back asleep because I was shocked. I couldn't believe Stan felt comfortable jerking off with me in the bed beside him. When Stan woke up, he seemed refreshed, and I was still in shock. So I went home and never said anything or even asked."

"That's crazy." He said as he walked toward me. He lifted me up and placed me on my bed. He unwrapped my towel and spread my legs apart. He was in between my legs, looking at Kay-Kay in awe.

"Everything okay?"

"I've heard my black friends talk about women with fat pussies, and I finally know what they are talking about. You have a pretty fat pussy. But what I like the most is that it's naked, screaming, Hello!"

"Okay." I heard Dustin moaning. As his tongue was caressing my core. I felt the tip of his tongue playing with my bud. He put his entire mouth over Kay-Kay and started sucking on her as if he was sucking for honey; she became his little honeypot. I grabbed his head, bent my legs, and rested my feet on his back. I started fucking his face, and all I could hear was him saying, "Mmmhmm."

"Oh shit. Right there, Dustin, right there." He was hitting my G-spot. "Oh shit! Right there, don't stop. Oh, oh shit! Dustin!" As he continued to tongue fuck me. The next thing I knew, my body was shaking and jerking. I began to orgasm, and then I squirted all over his face.

"And you taste good." He said as he kissed my inner thigh. I could see his dick was hard as a sword. Instead of playing around at the entrance, he slid right in. This young white man was doing his thing. He lifted me up and rolled onto his back; I was now on top. I was slightly bent over, so he was sucking on my breasts as I rode him. The way he sucked on my breasts turned me on; I could feel Kay-Kay getting wetter as I rode. I felt myself starting to orgasm again, but then he flipped my ass over, so I was back on the bottom, but on my stomach. He arched my hips for me and entered from behind. He fucked me, and I fucked him back. He had to slow down his strokes. "Shit!"

"Right there. Don't stop." This John Cena look-alike was doing the damn thing. But he was still slowing down. "Don't slow down."

"I can't help it." He said, slowly picking up the speed. "Oh shit." He said.

"Right there, I said as I threw it back at him. He began picking up the speed to the point where I stopped moving. He held onto my hips and fucked me until he couldn't anymore. Finally, he pulled out and came on my ass.

"All I need is five minutes," he said.

"Well, shit, I need." Then, before I could complete my sentence, I felt him wipe the cum off my ass with a towel, and he started tongue fucking me from behind. "Well, alrighty then."

"Sit on my face." He lay on his back underneath me, so all I had to do was squat over his face, but I got on my knees and fucked his face until I squirted all over it.

"Get on top."

"Does eating pussy make you hard?"

"I think it's just yours because I've never gotten hard off eating pussy before."

"There's a first for everything," I said as I sat down on his hard dick in reverse cowgirl position. I grabbed Dustin's ankles and rode him the way he fucked me. He stuck a finger up my ass, and that turned me on. He finger fucked my ass as I rode his dick. "Oh shit. I'm about to cum."

"Keep it right there and like that." He said, and I did. He pushed me off of him as he was about to cum.

"Well damn," I said as I fell on my face with my ass in the air. "That was good." I heard him snoring. I went back into the bathroom and took another shower. Dustin spent the night. He woke up early enough to leave, shower, and change clothes. We had lunch together almost daily, unless I had lunch with the bosses. Some days we would just go to my place and fuck and then return to work. Nobody knew about our little office fling, which continued for a year.

After that year, Dustin would call and come over occasionally, or I would go to his place. He even came to my surprise 30th birthday party.

COMPUTER I.T. GUY

We were getting a whole new server in our office. The bosses were getting frustrated every time our system froze or shut down. I must say, one of the bosses was very computer-literate and knew some people. Those same people recommended this company, and the bosses went with it. Of course, my job was to understand what was happening and pay them. I contacted Allen, who would be doing the work, and another gentleman. Still, Allen was the primary contact and, of course, their billing department.

It was time for them to come in and see what they were working with and what they would be replacing. So the bosses came into my office with Allen. "Kayla, are you busy?"

"No, come on in." I couldn't believe it. Allen looked exactly like Chico DeBarge, but he was a little taller. How did I know? He was in my face because I was in the front row at one of his concerts.

"Alan, this is Kayla. She is our office manager," my boss said.

Extending his hand to shake mine, he said, "Hi, Kayla, I feel like I already know you."

"Ditto." I was in complete fucking awe. Kay-Kay started throbbing, and I felt she was a little wet.

"Anything you need, you go to her."

"Anything I need?" Allen asked, with a seductively strange look, still holding my hand.

"Yes, anything." My boss replied. "Let me show you where the server is; it's not far from here."

"It's the door behind you," I said, pointing with my other hand.

"You can leave your things in her office; she doesn't mind." My boss said. How the fuck does he know I don't mind? Every now and then, I like to close my door.

"That's okay; I need this bag, so I'll take it with me." I guess he read my facial expression. Nice meeting you, Kayla."

"Nice to meet you as well, and I'm here in my office if you have any questions."

They both headed out, and Dustin came in.

"You want to go fuck?" I mean, you want to go to lunch?"

"You're funny, but I'm ordering in."

"All I have to do is close and lock the door, and we can fuck in here."

"We have people here working on the server, so I need to be available, and besides, we haven't fucked in a year. You hit a dry spell?"

"I just haven't had any good pussy, and I need some, so are we good for lunch?"

"That would be a no because I'm good; please leave my office?"

"Oh, it's like that now?"

"You know we are good. I have much work to do before I go on vacation."

"Where are you going, and who are you going with?"

"I'm going with Tionne and Breezy, and we're going to Barbados. Why are you asking?"

"Just being nosey. Ok, so I'll see you later. But, wait, where are you ordering lunch from?"

"You paying?"

"Yes, I can pay, but what are you ordering?"

"I'm ordering from the sushi spot."

There was a knock at my door; Allen said, "Excuse me, but can I check your computer for something?"

"Sure, just let me log out of what I'm doing."

"No problem."

"Are you going to get what you normally get from the sushi spot?" Dustin asked.

"Yes."

"Okay, so I'll go ahead and order and bring it to you when they deliver."

"Thanks, Dustin," I said as I was focused on what was on my computer screen."

Then, looking at Allen, "Is this going to take you long?"

"No, we just need to check everyone's computer. Is that your boyfriend?"

"If he is or isn't, I don't think that's any of your business."

"I apologize. I should have asked if it was okay to ask." Then, looking at the pictures on my desk, I said, "I'm going to take a guess that you're single."

"Did the pictures give that away?"

"Yes, they did. And if you would like to know, I'm a single dad; I have a daughter."

"Interesting. Okay, I'm done." I got up from my chair and sat in the chair in front of my desk. My boss then knocked on my door. "Kayla, we are headed out to a business meeting. We may return, but please show and give Allen whatever he needs."

"No problem." My boss left.

"You heard that?"

"Heard what?"

"Your boss told you to give me whatever I needed," he said with a devilish grin.

"Yes, he did."

"Well, there is one thing that you can give me."

"And what might that be?"

"Some pussy and your number." He said without skipping a beat as he looked at the computer screen. I was shocked, but the orifice between my legs felt like it had a slow drip.

"I don't know about the pussy part, but I have a business card on my desk with my cell phone number on it."

"That's fine. My coworker is still here, checking the other computers. I have to head back to our main office and work from there. I'll be back tomorrow, and be sure to wear a skirt or dress to work." He casually said as he got up and walked out of my office.

The next day was my early day; I got to the office two hours before everyone else to finish payroll for over five hundred employees. To my surprise, Allen came in about 15 minutes after me, and yes, I was wearing a skirt. "Good morning, Kayla. How are you this morning?"

"Good morning, I'm good. How are you?"

"Pleased," he said, smiling.

"And why are you pleased?"

"You wore a skirt. May I come in?"

"Sure." He walked in and closed the door behind him. Did I hear a click?

"Your bosses did say that you came in early today. So I figured I'd come early and get started, so we aren't here and in the way." He headed my way.

"Okay, but was there a reason you needed to close and lock my door?"

"Trust me," he said, still walking towards me. He got to my chair, spun it around, and then knelt. He hurried me down on the chair and pulled my skirt up. "Oh, no underwear, I like that." He then draped one leg over his shoulder and bent the other. He spread my lips apart and took long, deep licks of Kay-Kay, who was moist. "Dame," he said mid-lick and started to suck on my clit. He then put Kay-Kay in his mouth and continued to suck on her. "Grab my head with both hands." And I did. He held my hands and helped me push his face further into Kay-Kay. He continued to lick and suck, and I fucked his tongue like I was riding his dick. Somehow, I was entirely out of the chair, and he was on his back on the floor, and I was literally riding his face. I bent over so my hands were on the floor, no longer holding his head. Again, I was fucking his tongue. I fucked his tongue until my lower body went numb. As his hands were free, I could feel his body moving around; I heard his zipper unzip, and then he stopped conversing with Kay-Kay. He slid from underneath me and helped me up from behind. He moved the chair out of the way and bent me over my desk. When I looked back to see what he was doing, he put on a condom.

He turned me around and sat me on the edge of my desk. He had me leaning back on my elbows with both legs bent. His dick was long and thick. There was no teasing; he went right in. He was looking into my eyes as he was fucking me, and I knew I had to look away; before I could close my eyes, he came in for a kiss. I turned my head, and he kissed my neck. I was about to orgasm, and he collapsed on top of me before I could. I needed to get that nut. "Can I ask you something?"

"Sure," he said, out of breath.

"Could you go down on me for like two minutes?"

"Yes, I can." He started licking, and I started rubbing. I got my nut as he began sucking on my clit. The faster I stroked, the harder he sucked, and I could feel myself about to bust that nut, and damn it, that was a well-deserved nut.

After we were done, I went into the bathroom to freshen up. Then I returned to my office, sprayed some Lysol, and got to work. I still had an hour to myself in the office and let the sex smell fade before people started entering the office.

It took Allen and his guy a week to do the work, and on the days I came in early, I made sure Dustin did too. After they were done, Allen called me a few times after hours on my cell, and we had dinner a few times, but we didn't have sex again.

SIDE CHICK

So, I met Bill over the phone. As the office manager, I placed the calls when anything went wrong with the computers, water coolers, or printers. One of our printers was down, so I called the company that serviced our printers. Every time I called, I always got Bill. I'd schedule the appointment, and he'd send someone out. It reached the point where I would only talk to Bill, even if someone else could help me. We ended up exchanging personal numbers. We both worked in the city but got off at different times. One day, I was getting my hair done, and he came to the salon and waited for me. After I was finished, we walked around before heading to our trains. Bill was about six feet four inches tall, slim and muscular, with a milk chocolate complexion. After a few phone conversations, I discovered he was in an eight-year relationship. They had no kids together, but his girlfriend did have a daughter. I want to say they were in a good space. But one day, one of our conversations took a turn, for I won't say the worst, but it took a turn. I was home relaxing and drinking a glass of wine when he called. "Hello."

"Hey, Kay, what's up? What are you up to?"

"Nothing, just drinking a glass of wine. What are you up to?"

"I was just sitting here thinking about you sitting on my dick."

I spit the wine out, "Say what now?"

"You heard me."

"I don't think you can handle me and what I have. And why are you thinking about me sitting on your dick? Don't you have a girlfriend?"

"Yes, I do, but I find you attractive, and so does my dick."

"Wow, Bill!"

"We are honest with each other, so I don't see the problem."

"The fact that you have a girlfriend is the problem."

"So you going to come to ride this dick or what?"

"When?"

"Tonight, hop on the train and come to Brooklyn."

"I'm staying over if I do come."

"No problem, just bring your ass here and get on this dick."

"I'm going to drive; give me an hour. Then, text me your address." I finished my glass of wine, jumped in the shower, and shaved. By the time I was done, he had texted me the address. After getting dressed, I packed an overnight bag and headed out. It took me thirty minutes since there was no traffic. When I got in front of his building, I called him, "I'm looking for parking."

"I'll come down."

"Ok, I see someone pulling out, so I will grab this spot. I'm across the street from your building." I was out of the car when he got outside. He walked up to me and hugged me. Then, we headed inside the building to his apartment. When we got inside, he showed me around, then led me to his bedroom.

"Get comfortable," he said as he took off his sweatpants.

He took off my clothes. "Can I get a T-shirt?"

"For what?" He pulled me into his arms and started kissing me on my neck. I could feel his manhood getting hard. My eyes widened because I heard Kay-Kay say, *"Bitch is that a dick or a mini log?"* He sat on the bed with me between his legs. He played with Kay-Kay. "shit, she's fat and wet." She was both.

"Yeah, but do you know what to do with her?" He stood up, threw me down on the bed, and pulled down his pants. "What's that?" I screamed. His dick was the same complexion as he was, chocolate. It looked like the top of a Snickers bar; it was a good twelve inches, maybe longer, and as thick as my wrist and my wrists, better yet, put three Snickers bars next to each other, and there's the width. And he was hard. My God! All I kept thinking was that it would not fit; I was wrong. As he inched his dick inside Kay-Kay, I took a deep breath. "Shit!"

"What's wrong? Am I hurting you?"

"No, you are not hurting me." He wasn't, but his dick was piercing through my chest and hitting my uvula, the thing dangling in the back of my throat. Then he started picking up the pace. When I say he was giving me that D! He was indeed. She was gripping it, too. Ok, Kay! He was now lying on top of me, moving his hips in and out. "Shit!"

"You good?"

"Yes, I am." He then grabbed me into his arms and rolled over so I was on top. As he was still inside me, I could say that his dick was now really touching my uvula. I had to get up, squat, and bounce up and down on his dick. He named me Jackrabbit after that. I must say I jackhammered us both to sleep. The following day, I woke up to him rubbing his hard dick on Kay-Kay, and this bitch was wet and ready for him to enter. He gently shoved his way in. He grabbed my waist and pounded me out from behind. I threw it back at him from the side. We fucked until we both came. I could barely walk to the bathroom to shower, but I made it. I showered and got dressed while he went into the shower. We left together. He walked me to my car, and before I got in, he gave me the keys to his apartment and told me to meet him back there after I got off work. I got off before him. Bill wanted me there and ready for him when he got home. I was. Round three was that night.

Before I left the following day, I gave him back his keys, but he wouldn't take them. "Hold on to them, so whenever I want you to come over, or you want to come over, you can let yourself in."

"Are you sure? I mean, you do have a girlfriend."

"If I weren't sure, I wouldn't give you the keys. But I trust you will call to ensure I'm home alone when you want to come over."

"If you say so." I hugged Bill, got into my car, and went to work. We spoke five times that day, and the printers were all working fine.

Bill and I continued to fuck with each other for years. We were both into video games. When I would mention that I was about to get a game coming out or a new gaming system, he'd call and tell me to come over or ask me to go to his place because there was something there for me. Either the game or the latest gaming system. On Sundays, I even went to his home to watch football; we watched Monday Night Football at my place. He also had a key to my apartment. I also liked expensive bags and sneakers; whenever I went shopping, he was with me, and I never had to come out of my own pocket. I'd always ask him why he bought me things; he told me I deserved it, and it was more for my pussy than me. He would ride with me when I'd go to my mother's to visit. If I stayed there on the weekend, he'd drive up after work on Friday, we'd go to the mall on Saturday, and he'd go back home, and on Sundays, I'd drive to his place. Yes, he was still with his girlfriend. I was the side chick with wifey privileges. The kicker, he and his girlfriend were trying to have a baby and weren't successful. We weren't trying to, and we were successful.

Bill and I clicked, and everything was good, but he was in a relationship. He had been in one for a long time. The one thing, well, two things, I didn't want to ever be a side chick, but I got comfortable. I was really comfortable, to the point of settling. I didn't want to get pregnant in any situation; I was so relaxed that I got pregnant. I wanted to laugh, but not really; I thought about all the times I fucked raw and didn't get pregnant; now, look at me. So, I guess the streak had to come to an end. Here's where it gets a little tricky. He wanted a kid but wasn't successful with his current girlfriend, and they were trying. I don't know how he would tell her he cheated and got me pregnant, but I guess he'll figure it out. I'm against abortions, so we talked and cried about the situation.

This might sound crazy, but I had no problem with him still being in the relationship he was in, just as long as he helped financially and spent time with our child. He had no problem with that. He ended up coming with me to all of my doctor's appointments. I wasn't expecting him to do that, but he did. I lived in a two-bedroom apartment. He painted, put the crib in the second bedroom, which became the baby's room, and even helped me decorate. I discovered he hadn't been with his girlfriend in my sixth month. He said he came clean, and she wasn't with it. Shit, I don't blame her. Hey, shit happens.

It was time for the baby shower, and he made sure I invited his family, which I did. And they all came. I had met his sister before at his place, and she and I just clicked and became friends. I ended up meeting his entire family because she invited me to a BBQ they were having. Yes, he knew I had been asked and that I was going to be there. I was introduced to his girlfriend as his sister's friend. He and his sister were close and would cover for each other regardless of whether their actions were right or wrong. Anyway, the day my water broke, we were at my apartment. He took me to the hospital and was in the delivery room when I gave birth. We had a baby girl. She just turned six, and we co-parent without any problems, and occasionally we fuck.

I couldn't believe that something that big could come out of me. I knew big things could come inside if I could adjust, but they were never out of me. Although I must say that we had our share of fun before Kayla had a baby. We did have a little fun after she had her baby. I know she will eventually get bored with Bill, but when? Until then, I'll wait.

There were a few others I fucked after having a baby. When my daughter was six, I met a guy online who was sexy. He was six feet five inches, a basketball player; what's new? And he was nasty but in a good way. We would get together just to fuck. He would be fucking me, and he'd ask me to spit in his mouth. I ain't never did anything like that. No, he never spat in my mouth, and I didn't ask him to. We would have anal sex, and every time I'd put his dick in my ass, he'd always ask where his dick was. He was always shocked when I'd tell him in my ass but would keep going. It was funny when he came because he would be on his knees, shaking. After he stopped shaking, it looked like he was suspended mid-air, but kneeling behind me. It was the funniest thing.

Another guy I fucked was so eager to fuck me. I jerked him off the first time as he sucked on my tittie. His dick was tiny. I only used my thumb, index, and middle fingers to jerk him off. He wasn't big enough for me to use my hand. After about fifteen minutes of jerking him off, he announced that he was done. When we finally fucked he was moving in a circular motion, so I didn't feel anything, even when I tried to move with him. That was the last time.

I went back to fucking Bill. Kay-Kay was okay with it, and I was used to him.

My name is Kayla, and her name is Kay-Kay, and these were our tales worth telling. When I said we had a time, baybe, we had a time. I wonder what my heart would say about these events, cause my mind was with Kay-Kay.

EPILOGUE

These two only see eye to eye when Kay-Kay throbs. Our mind says, "Hmm, that looks good," and then sends a signal to Kay-Kay, and she jumps. Kayla then does what she has to do to fill both her and Kay-Kay's sexual appetite. They don't care about love —well, they do, but not as much as I do. If they did, they wouldn't have gotten into some of the shit they got themselves into.

I sometimes question their actions. Why do they act like that? Why, when I get involved, do they not listen to me? The heart knows best, right? If they listen to me, they might find the love and sex they deserve as opposed to having sex and falling for the wrong person or thing. I wonder where Kayla picked up this type of behavior. Her mother wasn't like that, but her father, on the other hand, was a womanizer. Could she have followed in his footsteps? Her brother's relationships were all long-term relationships. I yearn for love, and I know that Kayla does as well, but what was her issue? Did she or was she suffering from childhood trauma? Was she not able to recognize true love when it was in front of her? Did she not know what love looked like? Were the sexual escapades her coping mechanism?

We all need to be on the same page, and I was going to help whether or not she and Kay-Kay cared. Kayla, Kay-Kay, heart and mind were going to work together. I need a way to get us on track. Now, how am I going to do that?.